Isabella Macdonald Alden

Ester Ried's AWAKENING

CREATION
HOUSE
BOOKS ABOUT SPIRIT-LED LIVING
LAKE MARY, FLORIDA

Copyright © 1992 by Creation House
All rights reserved
Printed in the United States of America
Library of Congress Catalog Card Number: 92-72777
International Standard Book Number: 0-88419-320-9

Creation House
Strang Communications Company
190 North Westmonte Drive
Altamonte Springs, FL 32714
(407) 862-7565

Originally published in 1870 as *Ester Ried*

Unless otherwise noted, all Scripture quotations are
from the King James Version of the Bible.

CONTENTS

INTRODUCTION

nder the pen name "Pansy," Isabella Macdonald Alden exerted a great influence upon the American people of her day through her writings. She also helped her niece, Grace Livingston Hill, get started in her career as a best-selling inspirational romance novelist.

As Grace tells it in the foreword to *Memories of Yesterdays*, her aunt gave her a thousand sheets of typing paper with a sweet little note wishing her success and asking her to "turn those thousand sheets of paper into as many dollars.

"I can remember how appalling the task seemed and how I laughed aloud at the utter impossibility of its ever coming true with *any* thousand sheets of paper. But it was my first real encouragement, the first hint that anybody thought I ever could write. And I feel that my first inspiration came from reading her books and my mother's stories, in both of which as a child I fairly steeped myself."

On another occasion, a few months before

Grace's twelfth birthday in 1877, Isabella had been listening to Grace as she told a story about two warmhearted children. As Isabella listened, she typed out the story and later had it printed and bound by her own publisher into a little hardback book with woodcut illustrations. She surprised her niece with the gift on her birthday. That was Grace's first book.

Isabella Macdonald was born November 3, 1841, in Rochester, New York, the youngest of five daughters. Her father, Isaac Macdonald, was educated and deeply interested in everything religious. Her mother, Myra Spafford Macdonald, was the daughter of Horatio Gates Spafford (1778-1832), author and inventor. Isabella's uncle, Horatio Gates Spafford Jr., penned the popular hymn "It Is Well With My Soul" after learning that his wife had survived a tragic shipwreck; his four daughters were lost at sea.

Isabella was taught at home on a regular daily basis by her father. As her guide and friend, he encouraged her to keep a journal when she was young and to develop a natural affection for writing. Under his direction she acquired the ease and aptness of expression for which her writings became known. When she was only ten, the local weekly newspaper published her composition titled "Our Old Clock," a story that was inspired by an accident to the old family clock.

That first published work was signed "Pansy." Isabella acquired that name partly because pansies were her favorite flower and partly because of a childhood episode. She tried to help her mother prepare for a tea party by picking all the pansies from the garden to decorate the tea table. Not knowing the flowers were to be tied into separate bouquets and put at each lady's place, Isabella carefully removed all the stems.

Years later, while teaching at Oneida Seminary, from which she had earlier graduated, Isabella wrote her first novel, *Helen Lester*, in competition for a prize. She won fifty dollars for submitting a manuscript that explained the plan of salvation so clearly and pleasantly that very young readers would be drawn into the Christian fold and could easily follow its teachings. She gave the prize money to her parents.

Isabella wrote or edited more than two hundred published works, including short stories, Sunday school lessons and more than a hundred novels. She had only one manuscript rejected, a story sent to a periodical. At one time her books sold a hundred thousand copies annually with translations in Swedish, French, Japanese, Armenian and other languages.

She usually wrote for a young audience, hoping to motivate youth to follow Christianity and the Golden Rule. The themes of her books focused on the value of church attendance; the dangers lurking in popular forms of recreation; the duty of total abstinence from alcohol; the need for self-sacrifice; and, in general, the requirements, tests and rewards of being a Christian.

Reading was strictly supervised for young people in that day, and Sunday schools provided many families with most of their reading material. Thus, Isabella's fiction received wide circulation because of its wholesome content.

Readers liked the books. Her gift for telling stories and her cleverness in dreaming up situations, plus just a little romance, held the interest of readers young and old. Isabella was known for developing characters who possessed an unwavering commitment to follow the Master. She portrayed characters and events that anyone might have encountered in a small American town during the last quarter of the nineteenth century.

One writer in *Earth Horizon* (1932) acknowledged that "whoever on his ancestral book shelves can discover a stray copy of one of the Pansy books will know more, on reading it, of culture in the American eighties [1880s] than can otherwise be described." Some of the customs of the times in which Isabella wrote may seem peculiar to readers today, such as the general impropriety of women speaking in meetings where men were present. But to understand the present culture, we need to know the beliefs and practices that have gone before.

Isabella believed wholeheartedly in the Sunday school movement. She edited a primary quarterly and wrote primary Sunday school lessons for twenty years. From 1874 to 1896 she edited *The Pansy*, a Sunday magazine for children, which included contributions from her family and others. An outgrowth of the magazine was the Pansy societies which were made up of young subscribers and aimed at rooting out "besetting sins" and teaching "right conduct."

For many years she taught in the Chautauqua assemblies and, with her husband, was a graduate of what was called the Pansy Class, the 1887 class of the Chautauqua Literary and Scientific Circle — the first book club in America. The Chautauqua assemblies were an institution that flourished in the late nineteenth and early twentieth centuries. They combined popular education with entertainment in the form of lectures, concerts and plays that were often presented outside or in a tent.

Throughout her career Isabella took an active interest in all forms of religious endeavors, but her greatest contributions came in her writings. She wanted to teach by precept and parable the lessons her husband taught from the pulpit, in Bible class and in the homes of his parishioners. Her writing was always her means of teaching religious and moral truths as she understood them, and her method was to tell a story.

Her husband, Gustavus Rossenberg Alden, was a lineal descendant of John Alden, one of the first settlers in America. He graduated from Auburn Theological Seminary and was ordained soon after his marriage to Isabella in 1866. He served as a pastor in churches in New York, Indiana, Ohio, Pennsylvania, Florida and Washington, D.C. The Aldens moved from place to place for health reasons and to be near their son, Raymond, during his years of schooling and teaching.

Amidst her many and varied responsibilities as a minister's wife, a mother and a prolific author, Isabella found time to play a significant role in her son's career as a university professor, an author and a scholar in Shakespearean literature.

Her final years were marked by a series of trials. In 1924, after fifty-seven years of marriage, Isabella's husband died. In that same year her last remaining sister, Marcia Macdonald Livingston, Grace's mother, died. A month later her only son, Raymond, died.

About two years later she fell and broke her hip. Although in much pain and discomfort she continued writing until the end. Her final letters were filled with thoughts of going Home: "Isn't it blessed to realize that one by one we shall all gather Home at last to go no more out forever! The hours between me and my call to come Home grow daily less...."

Isabella Macdonald Alden died August 5, 1930, at the age of eighty-nine in Palo Alto, California, where she and her husband had moved in 1901.

The following year *Memories of Yesterdays*, her last book, edited by Grace Livingston Hill, was published. In the foreword Grace describes her aunt:

"I thought her the most beautiful, wise and wonderful person in my world, outside of my home. I treasured her smiles, copied her ways and listened breathlessly to all she had to say....

"I measured other people by her principles and opinions and always felt that her word was final. I am afraid I even corrected my beloved parents sometimes when they failed to state some principle or opinion as she had done."

As Grace was growing up and learning to read, she devoured her aunt's stories "chapter by chapter. Even sometimes page by page as they came hot from the typewriter; occasionally stealing in for an instant when she left the study, to snatch the latest page and see what had happened next; or to accost her as her morning's work was done, with 'Oh, have you finished another chapter?'

"And often the whole family would crowd around, leaving their work when the word went around that the last chapter of something was finished and going to be read aloud. And how we listened, breathless, as she read and made her characters live before us."

Ester Ried's Awakening, originally published in 1870 as *Ester Ried*, was one of Isabella's earliest books and became her most popular. It was also believed to be her most widely helpful. According to the November 1893 issue of *The Rest Islander*, the book kept up its sales "with astonishing regularity" after more than twenty years of circulation.

Isabella received scores of letters thanking her for its message. The story illustrates beautifully her ability to search our hearts and awaken us to our inconsistencies. In this book as well as in other writings she hoped to stir up Christians, whether ministers or laypersons, young or old, who had become complacent in their devotion to Christ.

As we accompany Ester Ried on her spiritual journey, perhaps we will see ourselves a little more clearly as God sees us. And, like the thousands of families who read and were helped by Isabella Macdonald Alden's books in her day, we will be awakened by this special volume from the Alden Collection to "right feeling, right thinking and right living."

Deborah D. Cole

THE CHARACTERS

Ester Ried
Sadie Ried, Ester's sister
Alfred and Julia Ried, Ester's brother and sister, twins
Minnie, Ester's niece
Laura Ried, Ester's mother
Maggie, the Rieds' maid
Boarders:
    Edwin Hammond
    Miss Molten
    Mrs. Brookley
    Dr. Philip Van Anden
    Mr. and Mrs. Holland
    Harry Arnett
Florence Vane, Sadie's friend
Mr. Vane, Florence's father
Mr. Newton, merchant
Abbie Ried, Ester's cousin
John, the butler at Abbie's home
Nancy, the maid at Abbie's home
Ralph Ried, Abbie's father
Helen Ried, Abbie's mother
Ralph Ried Jr., Abbie's brother
Edwin Foster, Abbie's fiancé
Fannie Ames, a teacher
Dr. Stephen Douglass, new boarder
Dr. Downing, Abbie's pastor
Dr. Archer, physician
Dr. Parker, guest minister

CHAPTER I

ESTER'S HOME

ster hurried to and from the pantry, as the sun slipped toward the west. She had no end of things to do. The kitchen was long and wide, and many steps were needed to set everything in order. It was nearly teatime on a Tuesday evening, and most of the fifteen boarders were punctual to a minute.

Sadie, Ester's next younger sister, was still at the academy along with the twins, Alfred and Julia. Little Minnie, the darling of the family, most certainly was not. She was in the way, poking little fingers into every possible place where little fingers ought not to be. It was to her benefit that, no matter how warm and vexed and out of sorts Ester might be, she spoke to Minnie only in loving tones. Besides being a precious little blessing, Minnie was the child of Ester's older sister, whose home was far away in a Western graveyard. The little girl had been living with them since her babyhood three years earlier.

"Maggie, do hurry and finish your ironing! I shall *never* have tea ready if you don't help me — no, no, Birdie, don't touch!" Ester said in quite a different tone to Minnie, who had just laid her loving hands on a box of raisins.

"I *am* hurrying as fast as I can!" Maggie exclaimed. "But such ironing as I have every week can't be finished in a minute."

"Well, well! Don't talk — that won't hurry matters any."

Sadie Ried opened the door that led from the dining room to the kitchen and poked in her thoughtless young head, covered with shining brown curls. "How are you, Ester?"

She emerged fully into the hot kitchen, looking like a bright flower picked from the garden and quite out of place. Sadie's fresh, pink gingham dress and white ruffled apron — and even the schoolbooks swinging by their strap — awakened a smothered sigh in Ester's heart. Her own brown hair matched her everyday brown dress — rumpled.

"Oh, my patience!" she greeted Sadie. "Are *you* home? Then school is out."

"I guess it *is*," said Sadie. "We've been down at the river since school."

"Sadie, won't you come and cut the beef and cake and make the tea? I didn't know it was so late, and I'm nearly worn out."

"I would in a minute, Ester, only I've brought Florence Vane home with me, and she isn't at all well. In fact, they say she may be very sick," Sadie replied soberly. "I wouldn't know what to do with her in the meantime. Besides, Mr. Hammond said he would show me how to work my algebra if I'd go out on the piazza this minute."

"Well, *go* then — and tell Mr. Hammond to wait for his tea until he gets it!" Ester retorted.

"Here, Julia," she said, turning to the ten-year-old fair-haired newcomer to the kitchen. "Get away from that raisin box this minute. Go upstairs out of my way and take Alfred with you. Sadie, take Minnie with you. I can't have her here another instant. You can afford to do that much, perhaps."

"Oh, Ester, you're cross!" laughed Sadie, reaching for the little girl.

"Come, Birdie, Auntie Essie's cross, isn't she? Come with Aunt Sadie. We'll go to the piazza and ask Mr. Hammond to tell us a story."

And Minnie — Ester's darling, who never received other than loving words from her — skipped merrily off, leaving Ester with a heavy heart. They stung her, those words: "Auntie Essie's cross, isn't she?"

Back and forth, from dining room to pantry, from pantry to dining room, flew the quick feet. At last Ester spoke: "Maggie, leave the ironing and help me. It's time that tea was ready."

"I'm just ironing Mr. Holland's shirt," objected Maggie.

"Well, I don't care if Mr. Holland *never* has another shirt ironed. I want you to go to the spring for water and fill the table pitchers and do a dozen other things."

The tall clock in the dining room struck five, and the dining bell pealed out its summons through the house. The boarders gathered promptly and noisily — schoolgirls, half a dozen or more; Mr. Edwin Hammond, the principal of the academy; Miss Molten, the main teacher; Mrs. Brookley, the music teacher; Dr. Philip Van Anden, the young, new physician; Mr. and Mrs. Holland, who owned a

store; and Mr. Harry Arnett, Mr. Holland's clerk.
The noise subsided while Mr. Hammond asked a
blessing on the food, then the lively talk continued.

Maggie poured cups of tea for everyone, and Ester passed bread and butter, beef and cheese. Sadie
carried out overflowing dishes of blackberries and
chattered like a magpie — which she did everywhere and always.

"This has been a scorcher," Mr. Holland said. "It
was all I could do to keep cool in the store, and we
generally have at least a breeze there."

"It has been more than I could do to keep cool
anywhere," Mrs. Holland added, patting her brow
with her handkerchief. "I gave it up long ago."

Ester's lip curled a little at Mrs. Holland's
words. That woman had nothing in the world to
do from morning until night but to keep herself
cool. She wondered what she would have said
about the steaming kitchen, where *she* had spent
most of the day.

"Miss Ester looks as though the heat has been
too much for her cheeks," Mrs. Brookley said
laughing. "What *have* you been doing?"

"Something besides keeping cool," Ester answered curtly.

"Which is a difficult thing to do," Dr. Van Anden
affirmed.

"I don't know, sir. If I had nothing to do but that,
I think I could manage it."

The doctor looked directly at Ester. "I have
found trouble sometimes in keeping myself at the
right temperature even in January."

Ester's cheeks glowed even more hotly. She understood Dr. Van Anden's meaning and realized
her face was not composed.

No one knew what prompted Minnie to speak

just then. "Aunt Sadie said Auntie Essie was cross. Were you, Auntie Essie?"

The household laughed, and Sadie came to the rescue.

"Why, Minnie! You must not tell what Aunt Sadie says. It is just as sure to be nonsense as it is that you are a chatterbox."

Ester thought they would *never* finish their supper and depart, but the latest guest finally strolled away. She hurried to toast a slice of bread and brew a fresh cup of tea for Julia to take to their mother, who had complained of a sick headache.

Sadie hovered around the pale woman while she ate. "Are you truly better, Mother? I've been worried half to pieces about you all day."

"Oh, yes, Sadie, I'm better. Ester, you look dreadfully tired. Do you have much more to do?"

"Only to trim the lamps, make three beds that I hadn't time for this morning, get things ready for breakfast and finish Sadie's dress."

"Can't Maggie do some of those things?"

"Maggie is ironing."

Mrs. Ried sighed. "It's a good thing I don't have a sick headache very often, or you would soon wear yourself out. Sadie, are you going to the lyceum tonight?"

"Yes, ma'am. Your worthy daughter has the honor of being narrator tonight. Ester, can't you go? Never mind that dress — let it go to Guinea."

"You wouldn't think so tomorrow evening," Ester returned sharply. "No, I can't go."

At last the work was finished, and Ester escaped to her room. How tired she was! Every nerve in her body quivered with weariness. She was glad for the quiet of the pleasant little room. It boasted of low windows with a view toward the river and cozy furniture that Sadie had tastefully arranged.

Ester seated herself by the open window and looked down on the group lingering on the piazza below — looked *down* on them with her eyes and with her heart. She envied their seemingly easy, carefree life. She envied Sadie because of her daily attendance at the academy, a pursuit she had been forced to quit early in life to help the family. She envied Mrs. Holland the ribbons and laces which fluttered in the evening air. It was cooler now; a strong breeze had blown up from the river and freshened the air. As they sat below enjoying the breeze, the sound of their happy voices floated up to her.

What do they know about heat or cares or trouble? she thought scornfully, remembering all the weight of her eighteen years of life. She hated it, this life of hers — sweeping, dusting, making beds, trimming lamps, working from morning till night, with no time for reading, study or pleasure. Sadie said she was cross, and Sadie told the truth. She *was* cross most of the time, fretting with her everyday cares and burdens.

"Oh! If *only* something would happen! If I could have one day, just *one* day, different from the others. But, no, it's the same old thing — sweep and dust, clean up, eat and sleep. I hate it all!"

Didn't Ester have anything to be thankful for — something to give her peace, something to which she could look forward? She did, if only she had thought of it.

When Ester was a little girl in school, her teacher had told her about following Jesus. One night beside her bed she pledged to do just that. Somehow, though, in the years since, the joy of that pledge faded and was lost in her wearying routine of chores.

Ester was so benumbed by the sameness of her days and by her own inward looking that she never mentioned her Savior to anyone. Yes, Ester was asleep! She went to church on Sunday and occasionally to midweek services. She read a few verses in her Bible, sometimes, not every day. She knelt at her bedside every night and said a few words of prayer — and that was all!

She lay at night in the bed side by side with a younger sister who had no claim to a home in heaven, and she never spoke to her of Jesus. She worked daily side by side with a mother who, through many trials and discouragements, was living a Christian life, but Ester never discussed with her the future rest that was waiting for them. She met daily, sometimes almost hourly, a large household and never thought to ask them if they, too, were going home to God some day. She helped her little brother and sister with their geography lessons and never mentioned the Christ who wanted to be their friend. She often held the darling of the family in her arms and told her of Bo Peep and the Babes in the Wood and Robin Redbreast but never once of Jesus and His call to the tender lambs!

This was Ester, and this was Ester's home.

CHAPTER II

WHAT SADIE THOUGHT

adie Ried was the most cheerful — and most thoughtless — young creature of sixteen years that ever brightened and upset a household. She was merry from morning until night, with scarcely a pause in her constant babble of fun. When she did think, she thought only of herself. Sadie was not by any means miserably selfish. But she had been taught to see herself as useless when it came to housework. She was amazed when someone would ask her to help.

And this busy Saturday morning was just such an occasion.

"Sadie!" Mrs. Ried called. "Can't you come and wash up these baking dishes? Maggie is mopping, and Ester has her hands full with the cake."

"Yes, ma'am," said Sadie, appearing from the dining room, with little Minnie perched on her shoulder. "Here I am at your service. Where are they?"

Ester glanced up. "I'd go and put on another

dress first, if I were you."

Sadie looked down at her pink gingham with its ruffled apron and shining cuffs and laughed. "Oh, I'll just take off my cuffs and put on your huge apron that's hanging behind the door. Then I'll be ready."

"That's my clean apron. I don't wash dishes in it."

"Oh, bless your careful heart! I won't hurt it the least speck in the world. Will I, Birdie?" And she proceeded to wrap her tiny self in the long, wide apron.

"Not that pan, child!" exclaimed her mother. "That's a milk pan."

"Oh," said Sadie, "I thought it was pretty shiny. My, what a great pan! Don't you come near me, Birdie, or you'll tumble in and drown yourself before I could fish you out with the dishcloth. Where is that thing? Here it is — Ester, it needs a patch on it. There's a great hole in the middle, and it twists every way."

"Patch it then," said Ester dryly.

"Well, now I'm ready. Here goes. Do you want these washed?" She seized upon a stack of tins piled up on Ester's table.

"Do let things alone!" said Ester. "Those are my baking tins, ready for use. Now you've gotten them wet, and I shall have to go all over them again."

"How will you go, Ester? On foot? They look pretty greasy. You'll slip."

"I wish you would go upstairs. I'd rather wash dishes all morning than have you in the way."

"Birdie," said Sadie seriously, "you and I mustn't go near Auntie Essie again. She's a 'bow-wow,' and I'm afraid she'll bite."

Mrs. Ried laughed. She had no idea how sharply Ester had been tried with petty irritations all that morning, nor how bitter those words sounded to her. "Come, Sadie," she said. "What a silly child you are. Can't you do anything soberly?"

"I should think I might, ma'am, when I have such a sober and solemn employment on hand as dishwashing. Does it require a great deal of gravity, Mother? Here, Robin Redbreast, keep your beak out of my dishpan."

Meanwhile, Minnie had been seated on the table, directly in front of the dishpan.

Mrs. Ried looked around. "Oh, Sadie! What possessed you to put her up there?"

"To keep her out of mischief, Mother. She's Jack Horner's little sister and would have had every plum in your pie down her throat by this time, if she could have gotten to them. See here, kitten — if you don't keep your feet still, I'll tie them to the pan with this long towel. Then you'll have to go around all the days of your life with a dishpan clattering after you."

But Minnie was intent on frolicking. This time the tiny feet kicked a little too hard. The pan was sitting too near the edge. It lost its balance and over it went.

"Oh, my patience!" screamed Sadie, as the water splashed over her and down the white stockings onto her daintily slippered feet.

Minnie raised her voice, increasing the general uproar. Ester left the eggs she was beating and picked up the broken dishes.

Mrs. Ried's voice rose above the din: "Sadie, take Minnie and go upstairs. You're too full of play to be in the kitchen."

"Mother, I'm real sorry," said Sadie, shaking herself out of the great wet apron, laughing even then at the plight she was in.

"Pet, don't cry. We didn't drown after all."

"Well, Miss Sadie," Mr. Harry Arnett said as he met them in the hall on his way to the post office, "what have you been up to now?"

"Why, Mr. Arnett, there's been another deluge — just like Noah's flood — this time of dishwater, and Birdie and I are escaping for our lives."

He caught Noah's name and launched a new topic. "If there is one class of people in this world more disagreeable than all the rest, it is people who call themselves Christians."

"Why, Harry!" she answered, shocked.

"It's a fact, Sadie. You just think a bit, and you'll see it is. They're no better nor pleasanter than other people, and all the while they think they're right about everything."

"What has put you into that state of mind, Harry?"

"Some things that happened at the store yesterday. Never mind that part. Isn't it so?"

"There's my mother," Sadie said thoughtfully. "She is good."

"Not because she's a Christian though; it's because she's your mother. It's the same way with my mother. You'd have to look till you were gray to find a better mother than I've got, and she isn't a Christian either."

"Well, I'm sure Mr. Hammond is a good man."

"Not a whit better or more pleasant than Mr. Holland, as far as I can see. I don't like him half so well. And Holland doesn't pretend to be any better than the rest of us."

"Well," said Sadie gleefully, "I don't know many good people. Miss Molten is a Christian, but I guess she is no better than Mrs. Brookley, and she isn't. There's Ester; she's a member of the church."

"And does she get on any better with her religion than you do without it? Personally, I think you are considerably more pleasant to deal with."

Sadie laughed. "We're no more alike than a bee and a butterfly or any other useless little thing. But you're very much mistaken if you think I'm the best. Mother would lie down in despair and die, and this house would collapse at once, if it were not for Ester."

Mr. Arnett shrugged his shoulders. "I always liked butterflies better than bees," he said. "Bees sting."

"Harry," said Sadie, speaking more gravely, "I'm afraid you're almost an infidel."

"If I'm not, I can tell you one thing — it's not the fault of Christians."

At that moment Mrs. Holland tossed some letters down to Mr. Arnett from the piazza above and asked if he would mail them for her. Letters in hand, he bid good evening and left.

Florence Vane walked over from the cottage across the way — with slow, feeble steps — and sat down in the door beside her long-time friend.

Almost immediately Ester appeared: "Sadie, can't you go to the post office for me? I forgot to send this letter with the rest."

"Yes," said Sadie, "that is, if you think you can go that little bit, Florence?"

"I shall think for her," interrupted Dr. Van Anden, coming down the stairs. "Florence, you're out here tonight, with the dew falling and nothing to protect your head — I am surprised!"

"Oh, doctor, do let me enjoy this soft air for a few minutes."

"Positively no. Either come in the house or go home. You are being very unwise," he admonished, his brows furrowing over his dark blue eyes. "Miss Ester, I'll mail your letters for you."

"Why does Dr. Van Anden want to act like a simpleton about Florence Vane?" Ester asked this question later in the evening, when the sisters were alone in their room.

Sadie paused in her chatter. "Why, Ester, what do you mean? About her being out tonight? Why, you know, she ought to be very careful, and I'm afraid she isn't. The doctor told her father this morning he was afraid she would not live through the season, unless she was more careful."

"Fudge!" said Ester. "He thinks he is a wise man. He wants to make her out to be very sick, so that he may have the honor of helping her. She looks no worse than she did a year ago."

Sadie turned and faced her sister. "Ester, what is the matter with you tonight? You know that Florence Vane has consumption, and you know she is my dear friend."

Ester did not know what the matter was except that this had been the hardest day, from first to last, that she had ever known. She was rasped until there was no good feeling left in her heart to touch.

And little Minnie had given her the last irritation of the day. As she was being hugged and kissed with eager, passionate kisses, she had exclaimed, "Oh, Auntie Essie! You've cried tears on my white apron and put out all the starch."

Ester set her down hastily and vanished.

Ester was grumpy and miserable. Dr. Van Anden was one of her thorns. He crossed her path quite often, either with direct, searching words about self-control or with grave silence. She disliked him.

From her pillow Sadie watched her sister kneel down hastily in the moonlight and knew that she was repeating a few words of prayer. She thought of Harry Arnett's comments earlier that evening. With her heart still throbbing from the sharp words spoken about Florence, Sadie sighed a little and said to herself: I should not wonder if Harry were right.

Ester was so much asleep that she did not know — at least she did not realize — that she had dishonored her Master all that day.

CHAPTER III

FLORENCE VANE

ster was of the same opinion concerning Florence one evening a few weeks later. She was hurrying past Dr. Van Anden when he detained her. "I want to see you a moment, Miss Ester."

During these weeks Ester's sympathy had been roused. Sadie was sick — sick enough to awaken many anxious fears and sick enough for Ester to discover what a desolate house theirs would have been if her merry music were hushed forever. She discovered, too, how very much she loved her lively younger sister.

Ester had been very kind and attentive. But the fever was gone now, and Sadie was well enough to rove about the house again. Ester began to think that it couldn't be so difficult to have loving hands ministering to one's simplest want, to be cared for and petted every hour in the day. She was returning to her impatient, irritable life. She forgot how high the fever had been at night and how the young head had ached. She remembered only how weary she was, watching and ministering day and night. So when she followed Dr. Van Anden to the sitting room in answer to his "I want to see you, Miss Ester," it was a very sober, not altogether pleasant, face which listened to his words.

"Florence Vane is very sick tonight. Someone should be with her besides the housekeeper. I thought of you. Will you stay up with her?"

If any reasonable excuse could have been found, Ester would surely have said no, so foolish did this seem to her. Why, only yesterday she had seen Florence sitting beside the open window, looking very well. But then, she was Sadie's friend, and it had been more than two weeks since Sadie had needed watching at night. So Ester could not plead fatigue.

"I suppose so," she answered slowly. Upon which, the waiting doctor wheeled around and left her, turning back only to say: "Do not mention this to Sadie in her present state of body. I don't care to have her excited."

"Very careful you are of everybody," muttered Ester as he hastened away. "Tell her what, I wonder? That you are making much ado about nothing, for the sake of showing your astonishing skill?"

A few hours later in precisely this state of mind she entered the cottage and the quiet room where Florence lay asleep — and, for all Ester could see, sleeping as quietly as a young girl ever did.

"What do you think of her condition?" whispered the old lady who acted as housekeeper, nurse and mother to the orphaned Florence.

"I think I haven't seen her look any better than she does at this moment," Ester answered abruptly.

"Well, I can't say that she looks any worse to me either. But Dr. Van Anden is in a fidget, and I suppose he knows what he's doing."

The doctor appeared at eleven o'clock, stood for a moment by the bedside and glanced at the old lady, who was dozing in her rocking chair. He then approached Ester and spoke in hushed tones: "I can't trust the nurse's stamina. She has not rested and is exhausted. I want you to stay awake. If she" (nodding toward Florence) "stirs, give her a spoonful from that tumbler on the stand. I shall be back at twelve. If she awakens, you may call her father. Send the Miller boy from next door for me. I shall be around the corner at Vinton's."

Then he disappeared as softly as he had come. The lamp burned low by the window; the nurse slept on in her rocking chair; and Ester fixed her wide-open eyes on Florence. All the while she thought the doctor was merely creating a story which would go forth the next day in honor of his skill and faithfulness. Yet she would not sleep at her post, even though she believed in her heart that, were she sleeping by Sadie's side and the doctor quiet in his own room, all would go well until morning.

But the doctor's evident anxiety had driven sleep from the eyes of the old gray-haired man whose one darling lay quietly on the bed. He came in soon after the doctor had departed. "I can't sleep...I'm worried. Does she seem worse to you?"

"Not a bit," Ester said. "I think she looks better than usual."

"Yes," Mr. Vane agreed, in a hopeful tone, "and she has seemed perked up all day. But the doctor is quite down about her. He won't say a single cheering word."

Ester became more indignant. He might at least have let this old man sleep in peace, she thought sharply.

At precisely twelve the doctor returned. He proceeded directly to the bedside.

"How has she been?" he asked of Ester.

"Just as she is now." Ester's voice was dry, with a tinge of sarcasm.

Mr. Vane scanned the doctor's face eagerly, but it was grave and sad. Quiet reigned in the room. The two men at Florence's side neither spoke nor stirred. Ester kept her seat across from them. She grew every moment more certain of her position, and more provoked.

Suddenly the silence was broken. Dr. Van Anden bent his tall, slender frame over the sleeper and spoke in a gentle, anxious voice: "Florence." She neither stirred nor heeded. Again: "Florence." The blue eyes fluttered open slowly and wearily.

The doctor drew back quickly and motioned her father forward. "Speak to her, Mr. Vane."

"Florence, my darling," the old man said gently and lovingly.

His fair young daughter turned her eyes on him. But her words were not about him or anything around her. So clear and sweet they sounded that Ester, sitting across the room from her, heard them distinctly.

"I saw Mother, and I saw my Savior."

Dr. Van Anden sank upon his knees, as the drooping lids closed again. His voice was low and tremulous: "Father, into Your hands we commit this spirit. Your will be done."

In a moment more all was bustle and confusion. The nurse was awakened. The doctor cared for the poor childless father with the tenderness of a son, then he returned to send the Miller boy, who had been waiting downstairs, for help and to give directions for what was to be done.

Through it all Ester sat motionless, petrified with solemn astonishment. The angel of death had been there in that very room. She had been so sure of her own opinions that she did not know it until he had departed with the freed spirit!

Florence really had been sick then — dangerously sick. The doctor had not deceived them, had not magnified the trouble. But she could not be dead! Dead! Why, only a few minutes ago she was sleeping so quietly! Well, she was very quiet now. Could the heart have ceased its beating?

Sadie's Florence dead! Poor Sadie! What would they say to her? How could they tell her?

Sitting there, Ester had some of the most solemn, self-reproachful thoughts she had ever known. God's angel had been present in that room, and in what spirit had He found this watcher?

Dr. Van Anden passed quietly and quickly from room to room, until everything in the stricken household was set in order. Finally he stood by the chair where Ester was still transfixed. "I will go home with you now," he said gently, brushing his dark hair off his forehead. He seemed to understand just how shocked she felt.

They crossed the street in the silent darkness of the night. As the doctor slipped his key in the door, Ester whispered, barely able to speak: "Dr. Van Anden, I did not think — I did not dream — "

"I know," he nodded, his kind blue eyes smiling upon Ester. "It was unexpected. I thought she would linger until morning, perhaps through the day. Indeed, I was so sure that I ventured to keep my worst fears from Mr. Vane. I wanted him to rest tonight. For his sake now, I am sorry I did not prepare him. But 'at even, or at midnight, or at the cock-crowing, or in the morning' — we know not which. I thank God that to Florence it did not matter."

The following days were filled with great opportunities for Ester, if she had only known how to use them. Sadie's sad, softened heart into which grief had fallen might have been encouraged by a few skillful words. Ester might have turned her thoughts from Florence to Florence's Savior. She tried. She was more gentle than usual with her young sister. Once, when Sadie was lingering fondly over memories of her friend, Ester said awkwardly something about Florence having been ready to die and how she hoped Sadie would follow her example.

Sadie was surprised but answered gravely: "I never expect to be like Florence. She was perfect, or at least I could never see anything about her that wasn't perfection. You know, Ester, she never did anything wrong."

And Ester, unaccustomed to talking about matters of the spirit and confused with her own attempt, kept silence. She let poor Sadie rest upon the thought that it was Florence's goodness which prepared her for death, instead of the blood of Jesus.

So the time passed. The grass grew green over Florence's grave, and Sadie missed her indeed. Yet the serious thoughts became daily fainter, and Ester's golden opportunity for leading her to Christ was lost.

CHAPTER IV

THE SUNDAY LESSON

t was a quiet Sunday afternoon in October. Alfred and Julia Ried were studying their Sunday school lesson in the sitting room. They were generally together. As twins they had commenced life together and had journeyed so far side by side. They had a lot of activities during the week, and the Sunday school lesson stood a fair chance of being forgotten. So Mrs. Ried had made the rule that half an hour of every Sunday afternoon should be spent in studying the lesson for the coming week.

Ester sat in the same room by the window. She had been reading, but her book had fallen idly in her lap, and she seemed lost in thought. Sadie, too, was there, carrying on a whispered conversation with little Minnie, who was snuggled close in her arms. Cheerful bursts of laughter came every few minutes from the little girl. The idea of Sadie keeping quiet or of keeping anybody else quiet was certainly absurd.

"But I say unto you that ye resist not evil, but whosoever shall smite thee on thy right cheek, turn to him the other also," read Julia slowly and thoughtfully. "Alfred, what do you suppose that can mean?"

"Don't know, I'm sure," Alfred said, scratching his tousled blond head. "The next one is just as odd: 'And if any man will sue thee at the law, and take away thy coat, let him have thy cloak also.' I'd like to see me do that. I'd fight for it, I reckon."

"Oh, Alfred! You wouldn't, if the Bible said you mustn't — would you?"

"I don't suppose this means us anyway," said Alfred, unconsciously using the well-known argument of all those since Adam's time who have tried to slip away from gospel teaching. "I suppose it's talking to those wicked old fellows who lived before the flood, or some such time."

"Well, anyhow," said Julia, "I'd like to know what it means. Mother always gets called to stay with sick people. If she were here, we could ask her. She would know. I wish she would come home. I wonder how Mrs. Vincent is. Do you suppose she will die, Alfred?"

"Don't know — just hear this, Julia! 'But I say unto you, Love your enemies, bless them that curse you, do good to them that hate you and pray for them which despitefully use you and persecute you.' Wouldn't you like to see someone who did all that?"

"Sadie," said Julia, rising suddenly and crossing the room to where the frolic was going on, "won't you tell us about our lesson? We don't understand a bit about it, and I can't learn anything that I don't understand."

"Bless your heart, child! I suspect you know

more about the Bible this minute than I do. Mother was too busy taking care of you two when I was a little chicken to teach me as she has you."

"Well, but what can that mean — 'If a man strikes you on one cheek, let him strike the other too?' "

"Yes," Alfred chimed in, "and, 'If anybody takes your coat away, give him your cloak too.' "

"I suppose it means just that," said Sadie. "If anybody steals your mittens, as that Bush girl did yours last winter, Julia, you are to take off your hood and give it to her."

"Oh, Sadie! You don't mean that."

"And then," intoned Sadie, "if that shouldn't satisfy her, you had better take off your shoes and stockings and give them to her."

"Sadie," said Ester, "how can you teach those children such nonsense?"

"She isn't teaching me anything," interrupted Alfred. "I guess I ain't such a dunce as to swallow all that stuff."

"Well," said Sadie meekly, "I'm doing the best I can, and you are all finding fault. I've explained to the best of my abilities. Julia, I'll tell you the truth." For a moment her laughing face grew sober. "I don't know the least thing about it — and I don't pretend to. Why don't you ask Ester? She can tell you more about the Bible in a minute than I can in a year."

Ester laid her book on the window seat. "Julia, bring your Bible here," she said. "Now what is the matter? I never heard you make such a commotion over your lesson."

"Mother always explains it," said Alfred, "and she hasn't come back from Mrs. Vincent's. I don't believe anyone else in this house can do it."

"Alfred," said Ester, "don't be impertinent. Julia, what is it you want to know?"

"About the man being struck on one cheek — how he must let them strike the other, too. What does it mean?"

"It means just that. When girls are cross and ugly to you, you must be good and kind to them. When a boy knocks down another, he must forgive him, instead of getting angry and knocking him back."

"Ho!" said Alfred contemptuously. "I never saw the boy yet who would do that."

"That only proves that boys are naughty, quarrelsome fellows who don't obey what the Bible teaches."

"But, Ester," interrupted Julia anxiously, "was it true what Sadie said about my giving my shoes and stockings and hood to folks who steal something from me?"

"Of course not. Sadie shouldn't talk such nonsense to you. That's about men going to law. Mother will explain it when she goes over the lesson with you."

Julia was only half-satisfied. "Then what does that verse mean about doing good to them that — "

"Here, I'll read it again," interrupted Alfred. " 'But I say unto you, Love your enemies, bless them that curse you, do good to them that hate you, and pray for them which despitefully use you and persecute you.' "

"Why, that is plain enough. It means just what it says. When people are ugly to you and act as though they hated you, you must be very good and kind to them and pray for them and love them."

"Ester, does God really mean for us to love people who are ugly to us and to be good to them?"

"Of course."

"Well, then, why don't we, if God says so? Ester, why don't you?"

"That's the point!" exclaimed Sadie in her most roguish tone. "I'm glad you've made the application, Julia."

Now Ester's heart had been softening under the influence of these peaceful Bible words. She believed them, and in her heart there was a real, earnest desire to teach her brother and sister Bible truths. Left alone, she would have explained that those who loved Jesus were struggling in a weak, feeble way to obey these directions — that she herself was trying, hard sometimes, and that they ought to. But Ester had this mark against her — her whole life was so different from those plain, searching Bible words, that the youngest child could not help but see it.

Sadie's mischievous tones and evident relish of her embarrassment at Julia's question destroyed the self-searching thoughts. Ester stood up and eyed her sister haughtily. "Sadie, if I were you, I wouldn't try to make the children as irreverent as I myself was." Then she hurried from the room.

Dr. Van Anden paused for a moment before Sadie, as she sat alone in the sitting room that same evening. "Sadie, is there one verse in the Bible which you have never read?"

"Plenty of them, doctor. I started reading the Bible through once but stopped at some chapter in Numbers — the thirtieth, I think, or some place where all those hard names are. But why do you ask?"

The doctor opened a large Bible which lay on the table before them and read aloud: " 'Ye have perverted the words of the living God.' "

Sadie looked puzzled. "Now, doctor, what possessed you to think that I had never read that verse?"

"God counts that a solemn thing, Sadie."

"Very likely, but what then?"

"I was reading on the piazza when I heard the children ask you for an explanation of their lesson."

Sadie laughed. "Did you hear that conversation, doctor? I hope you were benefitted." Then more seriously she asked: "Dr. Van Anden, do you really think that I was perverting Scripture?"

"I certainly think so, Sadie. Weren't you giving the children wrong ideas concerning the teachings of our Savior?"

Sadie was quite sober now. "I told the truth at least, doctor. I don't know anything about these matters. People who profess to be Christians do not live according to our Savior's teaching. At least *I* don't see any who do. It seems to me that those verses the children were studying cannot mean what they say, or Christians would surely try to follow them."

In answer the doctor turned the leaves of the Bible again and pointed with his finger to this verse, which Sadie read: " 'But as he which has called you is holy, so be ye holy in all manner of conversation.' "

After that he left the room.

Sadie read the verse over again. She could not help but understand that she had a perfect pattern to follow, if only she would choose to do so.

CHAPTER V

THE POOR
LITTLE FISH

other," inquired Sadie, appearing in the dining room one morning with Julia in hand, "did you ever hear of the fish who fell out of the frying pan into the fire?"

Without looking up from the great batch of bread she was molding, her mother answered with a question: "What mischief are you up to now, Sadie?"

"Why, nothing," replied Sadie innocently, "only here is the very fish so renowned in ancient history, and I've brought her for your inspection."

This answer brought Mrs. Ried's eyes around from the dough to Julia. As soon as she caught a glimpse of the forlorn little maiden, she exclaimed, "Oh, my patience!"

This same Julia was a specimen requiring great patience from anyone. The pretty blue dress and white apron were covered with great patches of mud. Morocco boots and neat white stockings were in the same direful plight. And down her face

41

muddy tears were streaming, for her handkerchief was also streaked with mud.

"I should think so!" laughed Sadie, in response to her mother's exclamation about patience. "The history of the poor little fish is this: Immaculate in her white apron and white stockings, she started for the post office with Ester's letter. She was tempted by a little girl with paper dolls. While our little girl was admiring them, the letter was mean enough to slip out of her hand and fall into the mud! That was the frying pan. Much horrified with this turn of events, the two wise young heads got together and conceived of washing the muddy letter in the creek! So to the creek they traipsed. While they sloshed around ankle deep in the mud vigorously carrying out their plan, the vicious little thing hopped out of Julia's hand and sailed merrily away downstream! So there she was, 'out of the frying pan into the fire,' sure enough! And the letter is now sailing to Uncle Ralph's in New York by an extraordinary route."

Sadie's nonsense was interrupted at this point by Ester, who had listened with darkening face to the story. "She ought to be thoroughly whipped, the careless little goose! Mother, if she ever needed punishing, she needs it *now*."

Then Julia's tearful sorrow blazed into sudden anger. "I oughtn't to be whipped. You're an ugly, mean sister to say so. I tumbled down and hurt my arm dreadfully, trying to catch your old hateful letter. You're just as mean as you can be!"

Between tears and cries and Sadie's laughter, Julia had managed to burst forth these angry sentences before her mother's voice reached her. "Julia, I am astonished! Is that the way to speak to your sister? Go directly to my room and put on dry clothes. Sit down and stay there until you are ready to tell Ester you are sorry and ask her to forgive you."

"Really, Mother," Sadie said, as the little girl stomped up the stairs, her face buried in her muddy handkerchief, "I think you've made a mistake. Ester is the one who should be sent to her room until she can behave better. I don't pretend to be good myself. But I must say it seems ridiculous to speak in the way she did to a sorry, frightened child. I never saw a more woeful, little figure in my life." She laughed again at the memory.

"Yes," said Ester, "you encourage her in all sorts of mischief. That's why she's so much trouble to manage."

Mrs. Ried looked distressed. "Don't, Ester," she said, "don't speak in that loud, sharp tone. Sadie, you shouldn't encourage Julia to be rude to her sister. Frankly I agree that Ester was hard on her. The poor child didn't mean any harm, but she must not be rude to anybody."

"Oh, yes," Ester said bitterly, "of course I am the one to blame; I always am. No one in this house ever does anything wrong except me."

Mrs. Ried sighed heavily, and Sadie turned away and ran upstairs, humming:

Oh, would I were a buttercup,
A blossom in the meadow.

Julia, in her mother's room, exchanged her wet and muddy garments for clean ones — and cried. She washed her face in the clear, pure water until it was fresh and clean — and cried again, louder and harder. Her heart was bruised and bleeding. She hadn't meant to be careless.

She had been dressed carefully that morning to spend the long, sunny Saturday with Vesta, one of her favorite school friends. She had intended to go directly to the post office with the small white treasure entrusted to her care. But those paper dolls were so pretty, and of course there was no harm in walking along and looking at them. How could she know that the hateful letter was going to tumble out of her apron pocket? Right there, too, the only place along the road where there was a tiny bit of mud!

Then she had honestly thought that a little clean water from the creek, applied with her smooth white handkerchief, would take the stains right out of the envelope. The sun would dry it, and it would travel safely to Uncle Ralph's after all. Instead of that, the hateful thing slipped right out of her hand and floated down the stream. Julia's sobs burst forth afresh.

Presently she took up her broken thread of thought: How very ugly Ester was. If she hadn't been there, her mother would have listened to her story of how very sorry she was and how she meant to do just right. Then her mother would have forgiven her, and she would have been dressed in her clean blue dress instead of her pink one and would have had her happy day after all. Now she would have to spend this bright day all alone. Her tears rolled down in torrents.

"Jule," called a familiar voice under her window, "where are you? Come down and mend my sail for me, won't you?"

Julia leaned out of the window and poured into Alfred's sympathetic ears the story of her grief and her wrongs.

"Just exactly like her," was his comment on Ester's share in the tragedy. "She grows crosser every day. I guess, if I were you, I'd let her wait a spell before I asked her forgiveness."

"I guess I shall," sputtered Julia. "She was meaner than anything, and I'd tell her so this minute, if I saw her. That's all the sorry I am."

And so the talk went. A few minutes later, Alfred was called to get Ester a pail of water, leaving Julia in solitude. She found her heart strengthened in its desire to tire everybody out in waiting for her apology.

The long, warm, busy day continued, until finally the overworked, weary mother toiled up the two flights of stairs in search of her young daughter. She hoped to sooth and help her. But Julia was in no mood to be helped. She hated to stay up there alone. She wanted to go down into the garden with Alfred. She wanted to go to the arbor and read her new book. She wanted to take a walk down by the river. She wanted her dinner right then. But to ask Ester's forgiveness was the one thing she did *not* want to do. "No, not if I have to stay here alone for a week — not if I starve!" she stamped her foot and grew indignant at the thought.

Alfred visited as often as his Saturday activities would permit and held emphatic talks with the little prisoner above, admiring her "pluck" and assuring her that he "wouldn't give in," not he.

"You see, I can't do it," said Julia, a gleam of satisfaction in her eyes, "because it wouldn't be true. I'm not sorry, and Mother wouldn't have me tell a lie for anybody."

So the sun drifted toward the west, and Julia at the window watched the academy girls heading home from their afternoon ramble. She listened to the clattering of dishes for tea in the dining room.

With no more tears to shed, she sighed and wished the miserable day were quite done, and she was sound asleep.

Only a few moments earlier she had received a third visit from her mother. Fresh from a talk with Alfred, she had answered her mother's question as to whether she wasn't now ready to ask Ester's forgiveness, with quite as sober and determined a "No, ma'am," as she had given all day.

Her mother had answered sadly, "I'm very sorry, Julia. I can't come up here again; I'm too tired. You may come to me, if you wish to see me anytime before seven o'clock. After that you must go to your room."

With this Julia had let her depart, only saying as the door closed: "Then I can be asleep before Ester comes up. I'm glad of that. I wouldn't look at her again today for anything." Then Julia was summoned once more to the window.

"Jule," Alfred said, with less decision in his voice now, "Mother looked awful tired when she came downstairs just now. And a tear was rolling down her cheek."

"It was?" said Julia in a shocked and troubled tone.

"She's had a time of it today," Alfred said. "Ester is too cross even to look at, and they've been working pell-mell all day. Minnie tumbled over the icebox and got hurt, and Mother held her for almost an hour. I guess she feels real bad about this; she told Sadie she felt sorry for you."

There was silence for a little while at the window above and from the boy below. Then he broke forth suddenly: "I say, Jule, hadn't you better do it after all — not for Ester, but there's Mother, you know."

"But, Alfred," interrupted the truthful and puzzled Julia, "what can I do about it? I must tell Ester I'm sorry, and that will not be true.

This question also troubled Alfred. It did not seem to occur to these two foolish young heads that Julia ought to be sorry for her own angry words, no matter how much in the wrong another had been. So they stood with grave faces and thought about it. It was Alfred who discovered a way out of the mist at last.

"See here — aren't you sorry that you couldn't go to play with your friend and had to stay up there alone all day and that it bothered Mother?"

"Of course," said Julia, "I'm real sorry about Mother. Alfred, did I honestly make her cry?"

"Yes, you did," Alfred answered earnestly. "I saw that tear as plain as day. Now, you see, you can tell Ester you're sorry, just as well as not. If you hadn't said anything to her, Mother could have made it all right. So of course you're sorry."

"Well," said Julia slowly, rather bewildered still, "that sounds as if it was right. Yet somehow — well, Alfred, you wait for me, and I'll be down right away."

So it happened that a very penitent little face stood at her mother's elbow a few moments after this. Julia's voice was very sincere: "Mother, I'm so sorry I made you such a great deal of trouble today."

And the mother turned and kissed the flushed cheek and answered kindly, "Mother will forgive you. Julia, have you seen Ester?"

"No, ma'am," she said more faintly, "but I'm going to find her right away."

Ester answered the troubled little voice with a cold "Actions speak louder than words. I hope you will show how sorry you are by behaving better in the future. Stand out of my way."

"Is it all done up?" Alfred asked a moment later, as she joined him on the piazza to take a last look at the beauty of this day which had opened so brightly for her.

"Yes," she sighed with relief. "Alfred, I never mean to be such a woman as Ester is when I grow up. I wouldn't for the world. I mean to be nice and good and kind like sister Sadie."

CHAPTER VI

SOMETHING HAPPENS

he letter which had caused so much trouble in the Ried family — especially in Ester's heart — was not an ordinary letter. Ester had written it to her cousin Abbie, her one intimate friend and Uncle Ralph's only daughter. These two who were the same age had corresponded almost from their babyhood. Yet they had never seen each other in person.

Ester's one great dream was to go to New York to her uncle's house to see and be with Cousin Abbie. It was as likely to be realized, she admitted, as a journey to the moon. New York was at least five hundred miles away. The money that was needed to carry her there seemed like a small fortune to Ester, to say nothing of the endless additions to her wardrobe which she would have to make before she would consider herself ready. So she contented herself — or perhaps it would be more truthful to say she made herself discontented — with endless dreams over what New York and her uncle's family and, above all, Cousin Abbie were like. She wondered if she would ever see them and why something had always prevented Abbie from visiting her. Would she like her as well as she did now if she could be with her? A hundred other confusing thoughts scurried about in her head.

Ester saw no benefit from this unhappy, restless dreaming of hers. She didn't realize that her very desires for a better life were tinged with impatience and envy.

Cousin Abbie was a Christian and wrote her some earnest letters. To Ester it seemed very easy for one to be a joyous, eager Christian when surrounded, as she imagined Abbie to be, by luxury and love. Into this very letter that poor Julia had sailed down the stream she had poured some of her inmost feelings.

"Don't think me devoid of all aspirations after something higher," the letter read. "Dear Abbie, you in your sunny home can never imagine how wildly I long sometimes to be free from my environment, free from petty cares and trials and vexations which are eating away my very life. Oh, to be free for one hour, for just one day, to follow my own tastes and inclinations — to be the person I believe God designed me to be, to fill the niche I believe He designed me to fill! Abbie, I hate my life. I don't have a single happy moment. It is all warped and unlovely. I am nothing, and I know it. I'd rather for my own comfort be like most of those who surround me — nothing and not know it. Sometimes I can't help asking myself why I was made as I am. Why can't I be a clod, a plodder, and drag my way with a simple good nature through this miserable world, instead of bruising myself at every step?"

Now it would be very natural to suppose that a young lady with a grain of sense left in her brains would in cooler moments have been glad for such a restless, unhappy, unchristianlike letter to be hopelessly lost. But Ester felt thoroughly angry that so much lofty sentiment, which she mistook for religion, was lost. Yet not one word of this rebellious outbreak was written simply for effect.

When Ester wrote that she hated her life, she was in earnest. "Oh, if something would only happen to calm me for just a little while!" she moaned in the solitude of her own room that evening. She was more in earnest than anyone has a right to feel on the subject — anyone who believes Christ has died to save her and that she has an eternal resting place ready and waiting to receive her. The letter had never reached its destination. But the merciful Savior, looking upon His poor, foolish lamb in tender love, hurried to send an answer to her wild, rebellious cry for help. She cried blindly, without a thought of the Helper who is sufficient for all human needs.

"Long looked for, come at last!" Sadie's voice rang through the dining room. A moment later, the young lady reached the pump room, holding up to Ester's view a dainty envelope, addressed in an even daintier hand to Miss Ester Ried. "Here's that wonderful letter from Cousin Abbie that you have sent me to the post office for three times a day for as many weeks. It reached here by way of Cape Horn, I'd say, by its appearance. It has been remailed twice."

Ester set her pail down, grabbed the letter and retired to the privacy of the pantry to devour it. For once she was oblivious to the fact that Sadie nibbled on bits of cake broken from the smooth, square loaf while she waited to hear the news.

"Anything special?" Mrs. Ried asked, pausing in the doorway.

Ester turned a flushed, eager face toward them, as she passed the letter to Sadie with permission to read it aloud. Surprised into silence by the unusual confidence, Sadie hurriedly grabbed the letter and started reading:

> My dear Ester:
>
> I'm in a grand flurry and shall not stop for long stories today but come to the pith of the matter immediately. We want you. That's nothing new, since we've been wanting you for many a day. But there is new decision in my plans, with new inducements this time. We not only want but must have you. Please don't say no to me this once. We're having a wedding in our house, and we need your presence. Every bride needs a sister, and you are the one we've chosen to play that role. Father says you can't be your mother's daughter and not have wisdom and charm. I'm very busy helping to get the bride in order, which is a work of time and patience, and I do so much need your aid. Besides, the bride is your Uncle Ralph's only daughter, so of course you ought to be interested in her.
>
> Ester, do come. Father says the enclosed fifty dollars is a present from him, which you must honor by letting it pay your fare to New York just as soon as possible. The wedding is set for the 22nd, and we want you here at least three

weeks before that.

Brother Ralph is to be first grooms-
man. He especially needs your assistance, as the bride has named you for her
first bridesmaid. I'm to dress — I mean,
the bride is to dress — in white, and
Mother has a dress prepared for the
bridesmaid to match hers, so that matter
need not delay or cause you anxiety.

This letter is getting too long. I meant
it to be very brief and to the point. I designed every other word to be 'come.'
But after all this I don't believe you'll
need so much urging to be with us at this
time. I flatter myself that you love me
enough to come if you can. So leaving
Ralph to give you directions about the
trains, I will run and try on the bride's
bonnet, which has just come home.

P.S. There is to be a groom as well as a
bride, though I see I've said nothing
about him. Never mind — you shall see
him when you come. Dear Ester, there
isn't a word of sense in this letter, but I
haven't time to put any in.

"Really," laughed Sadie as she concluded the
reading, "this is almost silly enough for me to have
written it. Isn't it splendid though? Ester, I'm glad
you are you. I wish I had corresponded with
Cousin Abbie. A wedding of any kind is a delicious
novelty, but a real New York wedding and a
bridesmaid besides — my! I've a mind to clap my
hands for you, seeing you are too dignified to do it
yourself."

"Oh," said Ester, from whose face the flush had

faded, leaving it actually pale with excitement and expected disappointment, "you don't suppose I am foolish enough to think I can go, do you?"

"Of course you will go, when Uncle Ralph has paid your fare, and more, too. Fifty dollars will buy a good deal besides a ticket to New York. Mother, don't even think of saying that she can't go. There is nothing to hinder her. She is to go, isn't she?"

"Why, I don't know," answered this perplexed mother. "I want her to, I am sure. But I don't see how she can be spared. She will need a great many things besides a ticket, and fifty dollars does not go as far as you imagine. Besides, Ester, you know I depend on you so much."

Ester's lips parted to speak. Had the words in her heart come forth, they would have been sharp and bitter ones — about never expecting to go anywhere or do anything but work.

But Sadie's eager voice was quicker than hers: "Oh, now, Mother, it is no use to talk in that way. I've quite set my heart on Ester's going. I never expect to have an invitation there myself, so I must take my honors secondhand. Besides, it is time you learned to depend on me a little. I'm two inches taller than Ester, and I've no doubt I shall develop into a remarkable person when she is where we can't all lean upon her. School closes this very week, you know, and we have vacation until the end of October. Abbie couldn't have chosen a better time. Whom do you suppose she is to marry? What an odd creature, not to tell us. Say she can go, Mother — quick!"

Sadie's last point was a good one in Mrs. Ried's opinion. Perhaps the giddy Sadie, at once her pride and her anxiety, might learn a little self-reliance by feeling a shadow of the weight of care which rested continually on Ester's shoulders.

"You certainly need the change," she said, her eyes resting on the young, careworn face of her eldest daughter. "But how could we manage about your wardrobe? Your black silk is nice, to be sure. But you would need one fancy evening dress at least, and you know we haven't the money to spare."

Then Sadie — selfish Sadie, who was never supposed to have one concern for others and very little for herself, who vexed Ester nearly every hour in the day — suddenly shone out brightly. She stood still and actually seemed to think for a full minute, while Ester jerked a pan of potatoes toward her and began peeling vigorously. Sadie clapped her hands then exclaimed, "Oh, Mother, Mother! I have it exactly. Why didn't we think of it before? There's my blue silk — just the thing! I'm tall, and she's short, so it will make her a beautiful train dress. Won't that do splendidly!"

The magnitude of this proposal silenced even Ester. To be appreciated, the reader must understand that Sadie Ried had never in her life possessed a silk dress. Mrs. Ried's best black silk had long ago been cut over for Ester; so had her brown and white plaid. There had been nothing of the sort to remodel for Sadie. This elegant sky-blue silk had been lying in its satin-paper covering for more than two years. It was the gift of a dear friend of Mrs. Ried's girlhood to the young beauty who bore her name. And it had been waiting all this time for Sadie to grow up so it could be cut out for her. Meanwhile she had settled for feasting her eyes upon it. She also gloried in the prospect of that wonderful day when she would sweep across the platform of the music hall with this same silk falling in beautiful blue waves around her. It had long since been decided that she would first wear it on her graduation day.

No wonder, then, that Ester was astonished into silence.

Mrs. Ried was the first to find voice for her thoughts: "Why, Sadie, my dear child, is it possible you are willing to give up your blue silk?"

"Not a bit, Mother. I don't intend to give it up the least bit in the world. I'm merely going to lend it. It's too pretty to stay poked up in that drawer by itself any longer. I've set my heart on its coming out this very season. Just as likely as not it will learn to put on airs for me when I graduate. I'm not at all satisfied with my accomplishments along those lines now anyway. So Ester shall take it to New York. And if she sits down or stands up or turns around or lacks one minute's peace while she has it on, for fear lest she should spot it or tear it or get it stepped on, I'll never forgive her."

At this harangue Ester laughed freely and happily, a rare activity for her. Somehow it seemed as if she really were to go, for Sadie had said in such a brisk, businesslike manner, "Ester shall take it to New York." Oh, if she only, only could go, she would be willing to do anything after that. She felt she must have just one little peep into the beautiful, fantasy world that lay outside that dining room and kitchen. Perhaps that laugh did as much for her as anything.

It almost startled Mrs. Ried with its sweetness and rarity. What if the change would freshen her and bring her back to them with some of the sparkles that danced in Sadie's eyes? But what if she should grow utterly disgusted with the monotony of their very quiet, very busy life and refuse to work in that most necessary treadmill any longer? So the mother argued and hesitated. And the decision, which would mean so much more than any of them knew, trembled in the balance. Let Mrs. Ried say once, "Oh, Ester, I don't think you will have to give it up," and Ester would have turned quickly to that pan of potatoes, and with a sneer she would have sharply forbidden anyone to mention the subject to her again.

Once more Sadie — dear, merry, silly Sadie — came to the rescue. "Mother, oh, Mother! What an endless time you are taking in deciding! I could plan an expedition to the North Pole in less time than this. I'm just wild for her to go. I want to hear how a genuine New York bride looks. Besides, dear Mother, I want to stay in the kitchen with you. Ester does everything, and I don't have any chance. I long to bake and boil and broil and brew things. Say yes, there's a darling."

Mrs. Ried looked at the bright, flushed face and thought how little the dear child knew about all these matters. How little patience poor Ester, who was so competent herself, would have with Sadie's ignorance. Finally she said with great hesitation, but actually she did say for all to hear: "Well, Ester, my daughter, I really think we must try to get along without you for a little while!"

And these three people really thought it was they who had decided the matter. Two of them were, at least in theory, believers in a "special Providence." But it never occurred to them that this little matter in all its details had been settled for ages.

CHAPTER VII

JOURNEYING

wenty minutes here for refreshments!"

"Passengers for New York — take the south track!"

"New York daily papers here!"

"Sweet oranges here!"

Amid the cacophony of discordant yells, the screeching of engines, the ringing of bells and the intolerable din of a merciless gong, Ester pushed and elbowed her way through the crowd. She was almost panting in her efforts to keep up with Mr. Newton, her nervous traveling companion and a merchant in the village. Mrs. Ried, on Dr. Van Anden's advice, had decided he would be a good escort for Ester since he was going to New York to buy goods for his store.

He hurried her through the crowd and the noise into the dining saloon and stood by her side while, obeying his orders, she poured down her throat a cup of almost boiling coffee. He seated her in the ladies' waiting room and ordered her not to stir

from that spot for any reason while he was gone;
he had just enough time to run around to the post
office and mail a forgotten letter. Then he vanished, and in the confusion of the crowd Ester was
alone.

She did not feel the least bit flurried or anxious.
On the contrary, she liked it, this first experience of
hers in a city depot. She wouldn't have let it be
known for the world to any of the fashionably at-
tired, much-at-ease travelers who thronged past
her. But the truth was, Ester had been having her
very first ride on the train!

Sadie had taken various little trips with her
school friends to adjoining towns to obtain school
books or music or to attend a concert or simply for
fun. And although Ester had spent her eighteen
years of life in a town which had long been an
express station, yet for lack of time or money or
inclination to take the little journeys within her
reach, she had stayed at home. Now she glanced at
herself in her perfectly neat, ladylike traveling suit.
She could catch a full view of it in the looking glass
across from her. The suit was becoming, from the
dainty veil fluttering over her hat to the gleaming
tips of her walking boots.

She emitted a complacent little sigh: I think I
look as much like a traveler as any of them. I'm
glad I'm not dressed like that pert-looking girl in
brown. It's ridiculous and in very bad taste to
travel in such a rich silk. She looks as if she thinks
only of her clothes. That's probably what she's
thinking about at this very moment.

Ester's face betrayed contempt and an air of su-
periority as she watched the bit of silk and ribbons.
Ester had a mistaken opinion of herself in this regard. She would have been indignant had anyone

told her that her pretended contempt for the rich,
elegant attire displayed around her was really the
result of envy. When she told herself she wouldn't
lavish so much time and thought and, above all,
money on mere outside show, it was mere nonsense.

The truth was, Ester had exquisite taste. Give
her the means and she would have glistened in silk
and sparkled in jewels. But she thought that her
bitter denunciation of fashion and extravagance in
this form was outward evidence of a mind ele-
vated far above such trivial subjects. She thus
looked down on those whom she considered to be
"butterflies of fashion."

In her flights into a "higher sphere of thought,"
this absurdly inconsistent Ester never once remembered her behavior, just exactly a week ago that
day: She had stormed around her otherwise peaceful home, almost wearing out her weary mother's
patience. She rendered the house intolerable to
Sadie and actually boxed Julia's ears. She did all
that because she could not have her blue silk, or
rather Sadie's blue silk, trimmed with netted fringe
at twelve shillings a yard but must do with simple
folds and a seventy-five-cent heading!

Such a two weeks as the last had been in the
Ried family! The entire household had joined in
the uproar caused by Ester's upcoming journey.

Mrs. Ried toiled early and late and made many
quiet little sacrifices to keep her daughter from
feeling too keenly the difference between her own
and her cousin's wardrobe. Sadie emptied her "finery" box and donated every article in it, giving
comic little lectures to each bit of lace and ribbons
as she smoothed and patted them and told them
they were going to New York.

Julia hemmed handkerchiefs and pricked her poor little fingers without complaint. Alfred ran errands with remarkable promptness. He confessed to Julia privately that he was in such a hurry to have Ester gone so he could see what it would be like for everyone to be in a good mood.

Little Minnie got in everybody's way, as much as a tiny creature could, and finally brought the tears to Ester's eyes. She sent everyone else into bursts of laughter by bringing a very smooth little handkerchief about six inches square and offering it as her contribution toward the traveler's outfit.

As for Ester, she was nervous and unbearably cross through the whole of it, wanting a hundred things which were impossible for her to have. She scorned not a few of the little trifles that had been prepared for her by generous, toil-worn fingers.

"Ester, I do hope New York or Cousin Abbie or somebody will have a soothing and improving effect upon you," Sadie had said with good-humored impatience only the night before her departure. "Now that you have reached the summit of your hopes, you seem more uncomfortable about it than you were even to stay at home. Do let us see you look pleasant for just five minutes, so that we may have something good to remember you by."

"My dear," Mrs. Ried had interposed, "Ester is hurried and tired and has had a great many things to try her today. It's not a good idea, especially when a family is about to separate, to say any careless or foolish words that we don't mean. I have a great many days of Ester's hard work to remember her by."

What a patient, tender, forgiving mother! Ester, asleep to her own faults, never once thought of the half-disgusted way in which she had performed much of her work. She only remembered, with a little sigh of satisfaction, the many cakes and pies she had baked that very morning to save her mother's steps. This was all she thought of now, but the day would come when she would be wide-awake.

Meanwhile the New York train, after panting and snorting several times to announce that the twenty minutes were about up, suddenly puffed and rumbled its way out from the depot and left Ester obeying orders. There she sat in the corner where Mr. Newton had placed her. She was calm on the outside, but in her heart brewed a perfect storm of vexation.

This comes from Mother's absurd fussiness in putting me in Mr. Newton's care, she fumed inwardly. She should have let me travel alone, as I wanted to. Now we shall not get into New York until after six o'clock! How provoking!

"How provoking this is!" Mr. Newton exclaimed, echoing her thoughts. He bustled in, red with haste and heat, and stood penitently before her. "I had no idea it would take so long to go to the post office. I am very sorry!"

He recovered his good humor, despite Ester's irritating silence. "What can't be cured must be endured, Miss Ester. It isn't as bad as it might be, either. We only have to wait an hour and fifteen minutes. I have some errands to do, and I'll show you the city with pleasure. Or would you prefer to stay here and just look at what is around you?"

"I definitely prefer not to risk missing the next train," Ester answered sharply. "So I think it will be wiser to stay where I am."

Mr. Newton responded to his own carelessness

with too much complacency to suit Ester's state of mind. But he took no notice of her hint other than to assure her that she needn't feel uneasy; he would certainly be on time.

Then he left her, sighing with relief; he frankly confessed to himself that he did not know how to take care of a lady. "If she were a package of goods that one could store or check and know that she would come out all right, why — but a lady. I'm not used to it. I could have caught that train easily, if I hadn't had to run back after her. But, bless me, I wouldn't have her know that for the world," he said as he walked down South Street.

The New York train had carried away the greater portion of the throng at the depot. Ester and the dozen or so people who occupied the great sitting room with her had relative quiet. The wearer of the condemned brown silk and blue ribbons was still there and awakened Ester's vexation even further by fluttering from seat to seat and from window to window like a bird in a cage.

Suddenly she addressed Ester in a happy little tone: "Doesn't it bore you dreadfully to wait in a depot?"

"Yes," said Ester, briefly and truthfully, despite the fact that she was having her first experience in that kind of boredom.

"Are you going to New York?"

"I hope so!" she exclaimed. "I'd have almost been there by now, but the gentleman who is supposed to be taking care of me had to rush off. He stayed just long enough to miss the train."

"How annoying!" answered the girl of the blue ribbons with a soft laugh. "I missed it, too, in such a silly way. I ran around the corner to get some chocolate drops, and a little matter detained me a few moments. When I came back, the train had gone. I was so sorry, for I'm in such a hurry to get home. Do you live in New York?"

Ester shook her head, thinking, That is just as much sense as I'd guess you to have — miss a train for a piece of candy.

Ester could not know that the chocolate drops were for the tiny sister at home, whose heart would be nearly broken if sister Fanny came home, after an absence of twenty-four hours, without bringing her anything. Nor could she know that the "little matter" which detained her a few moments was joining in a search for a twenty-five-cent bill. The ruthless wind had snatched it from the hand of a barefooted, bareheaded and almost forlorn little girl, who cried as if her last hope in life had been blown away with it. Failing to find the treasure, the gold-clasped purse had been opened, and a crisp, new bill had been taken out to fill its place. If Ester had known the circumstances, it probably would not have made any difference in her verdict.

The side door opened quietly just at this point, and a middle-aged man came in, carrying a tool-box in one hand and a tin pail in the other. Both girls eyed him curiously as he set these down on the floor. Taking short nails from his pocket and a hammer from his box, he tacked a piece of paper to the wall. From where she sat, Ester could see that the paper was small and that something was printed on it in close, fine type. It didn't look like an advertisement or even a notice of any kind. Her curiosity was piqued. Two tiny tacks held it firmly in its place.

Then the man turned and surveyed the occupants of the room, who were by this time giving undivided attention to him and his bit of paper. In a respectful tone he told them: "I've tacked up a nice little tract. I thought maybe while you were waiting you might like to read something. If one of you would read it out loud, all the rest could hear it." So saying, the man stooped and picked up his toolbox and his tin pail and disappeared, leaving those two or three strokes of his hammer to work for him through all time and meet him at the judgment.

But if a bombshell had suddenly dropped and laid itself in ruins at their feet, it could not have created a much more startled group than the tract-tacker left behind him. A tract — actually tacked up on the wall and waiting for some human voice to give it utterance! A tract in a railroad depot! How odd! How almost improper! Why? Oh, Ester didn't know; it was just so — unusual. Yes, but that didn't make it improper. No; but — then, she — it — well, it was fanatical. Yes, that was it. She knew it was improper in some way. It was strange that that very convenient word should have escaped her. This talk Ester held hurriedly with her conscience which was asleep, you remember. Just then it nestled as in a dream and gave her a little prick, but that industrious, important word *fanatical* lulled it back to its rest. Meanwhile there hung the tract, flapping in the summer air with the opening and closing of the door. Would no one give it voice?

"I'd sure like to hear it," an old lady said, nodding her gray head toward the little leaflet on the wall. "But I've packed up my specs and might as well have no eyes at all, as far as readin' goes, when I don't have my specs on. There's some young eyes 'round here though, one would think," she added, gazing around the room. "You won't need glasses, I should say now, for a spell of years!"

This remark — or hint — was directed squarely at Ester. The only answer it received was a shrug of the shoulder and an impatient tapping of her heels on the bare floor. Under her breath Ester muttered, "Disagreeable old woman!"

The brown silk rustled, and the blue ribbons rippled restlessly for a minute. Then their owner's clear voice broke the silence: "I'll read it for you, ma'am, if you would like to hear it."

The wrinkled face beamed, as the old woman turned toward the pink-cheeked, blue-eyed maiden. "That I would," she answered heartily, "dreadful well. I ain't heard nothing good, 'pears to me, since I started, and I've come two hundred miles. It seems as if it might kind of lift me up and rest me like to hear something real good again."

With the flush on her face a little heightened, the young girl crossed to where the tract hung. A strange stillness settled over the listeners as her clear voice rang out down the long room. This was what she read:

Dear Friend:
What is the foundation of your life? How do you hope to enter heaven? Is it by having the right opinions or ideas? Is it by belonging to a church? These may help you on your journey, but they will, in the end, amount to nothing.

You cannot stop here. Do you build your life on not wronging or hurting anyone, on doing no harm? Oh, that this might be true! You are honest and fair with everyone. You do not cheat or extort. You have a clear conscience toward God. That is commendable; yet it is not the thing.

Do you take part in the practices of your church — the Lord's supper, prayer and hearing and reading the Scriptures? Indeed, you ought to be doing these things, but they alone — without faith, mercy and the love of God — are nothing.

Are you zealous of good works? Do you do good to all people — the poor, the sick, the hungry, the fatherless? Is the stranger by your side a fellow pilgrim? Have you asked if he would be? Do you speak the truth as it is in Jesus? And does His Spirit influence your words? Then go and learn this truth again: "By grace are you saved through faith...not by works of righteousness which we have done, but of His own mercy He saved us."

Count all you have done as waste. Apply to Jesus just as the dying thief did, unless, after saving others, you lose your own soul.

Put all your hope in the blood of Jesus and in His Spirit. He bore all your sins in His own body on the cross. And then depend upon Him for every good thought and word and work.

During the reading of the tract, a young man had entered, paused a moment in surprise at the unusual scene, then walked quietly across the room and took the vacant seat near Ester. As the reader came back to her seat, with the pink on her cheek deepened into warm crimson, the newcomer greeted her:

"Good evening, Miss Fannie. Have you been finding work to do for the Master?"

"Only a very little thing," she answered, with a slight tremble in her voice.

"I don't know about that, my dear," the old woman said. "I'm sure I thank you a great deal. They're kind of startling questions like, enough to 'most scare a body unless you was trying pretty hard, now, ain't they?"

"Very serious questions, indeed," answered the gentleman to whom this question seemed to be addressed. "I wonder, if we were obliged to write truthful answers to each one of them, how many we would want others to see."

"How many would we want *Him* to see?" The old woman spoke with an emphatic shake of her gray head and a reverent emphasis of the pronoun.

"That is the vital point," he said. "Yet how much do we want man's approval rather than God's."

Then he turned suddenly to Ester and spoke in a quiet, respectful tone: "Is the stranger by my side a fellow pilgrim?"

Ester was embarrassed and confused. The whole scene had been a very strange one to her. She tried to think the blue-ribboned girl was dreadfully out of her sphere. But the questions following each other in such rapid succession were so very serious and personal and searching — and now this one. She hesitated and stammered and flushed like a schoolgirl. At last she faltered: "I — I think — I believe — I am."

"Then I trust you are wide awake and a faithful worker in the vineyard," he said earnestly. "These are times when the Master needs true and faithful workers."

He's a minister, Ester assured herself. She had recovered from her confusion enough to watch him closely. He folded the old woman's shawl for her, took her box and basket in his care and offered his hand to help her into the cars. The New York train had thundered in at last, and Mr. Newton presented himself. The passengers rushed and jostled each other out of the depot and into the train.

And the little tract hung quietly in its corner. The carpenter who had left it there prayed that God would use it and knew not then nor afterward that it had already awakened thoughts that would tell for eternity.

CHAPTER VIII

THE JOURNEY'S END

es, he's a minister, Ester repeated to herself with more conviction. Seated in the speeding train, directly behind the old lady and the young gentleman who had become the subject of her thoughts, she observed his actions and manner more closely. Mr. Newton was absorbed in the *Tribune* so she gave her undivided attention to the two. She could hear snatches of the conversation which passed between them, as well as note his courtesy when he brought her a cup of water and attended to all her simple wants. While stopped at a station, their talk became distinct.

"And I haven't seen my boy, don't you think, in ten years," the old lady was saying. "Won't he be glad though to see his mother once more? And he's got children — two of them."

"So the old home is broken up, and you are going to make a new one," her companion answered.

"Yes, and I'll show you everything I've got to remember my old garden by."

Her fingers shaking, she untied the string which held down the cover of her basket. Rummaging inside, she brought out a withered bouquet of common and homely flowers, if any flowers can be called homely.

"There," she said, holding the bouquet tenderly. "I picked 'em the very last thing out in my own little garden patch by the backdoor. Oh, many's the time I've sat and weeded and dug around them, with my boy sitting on the stoop and reading out loud to me. I thought all about just how it had been while I was picking these. I didn't stay no longer, and I didn't go back to the house after that. I couldn't; I just pulled my sunbonnet over my eyes and went down the street to where I was going to get my breakfast."

Ester felt very sorry for the poor homeless, friendless old woman. She would have been willing to do a good deal just then to make her comfortable. Yet she had to admit that that awkward bunch of faded flowers, arranged without the slightest regard to colors, looked rather ridiculous. She was surprised and not a little puzzled to see actual tears standing in the eyes of her companion as he handled the bouquet with such tender care.

"Well," he said after a quiet moment, "you are not leaving your best friend after all. Does it comfort your heart to remember that, in all your trials and separations, you are never called upon to bid Jesus good-bye?"

What a way he has of bringing that subject into every conversation, observed Ester wryly, who was now sure that he was a minister. Ester thought everyone who spoke freely about religious matters must be either a fanatic or a minister.

"Oh, that's about all the comfort I've got left."

This answer came from a full heart and eyes brimming with tears. "And I don't s'pose I need any other, if I've got Jesus left. I oughtn't to need anything else. Sometimes I get impatient — it seems to me I've been here long enough, and it's time I got home."

"How is it with the boy who is expecting you? Does he have this same friend?"

The gray head shook slowly. "Oh, I'm afraid he don't know nothing about Him, leastwise, not that he's said in his letters."

"Ah! Then you have work to do. You can't be spared to rest yet. I presume the Master is waiting for you to lead that son to Himself."

"I mean to. I mean to, sir," she said. "Sometimes I think maybe my coffin could do it better than I. God knows — and I'm trying to be patient."

Then the train whirred on again, and Ester missed the rest. But one sentence caught her attention. "Maybe my coffin could do it better than I." How sincerely she spoke, as if she were willing to die at once, if by that she could save her son. How earnest they both were, anyway — the wrinkled, homely, old woman and the cultivated, courtly gentleman. Ester squirmed inwardly — her conscience was arousing her to unaccustomed thought. These two were different from her. She was a Christian — at least she thought so, hoped so. But she was not like them. There was a very decided difference. Were they right, and was she all wrong? Wasn't she a Christian after all? At this thought she shivered. She was not willing to give up her title, weak though it might be.

Oh, well, she finally decided, she is an old woman, almost through with life. Of course, she looks at everything from a different point of view from what a young girl like me naturally would. As for him, ministers are always different from other people, of course.

Foolish Ester! Did she suppose that ministers have a private Bible of their own with rules of life set down therein for them, quite different from those written for her? As for the old woman, almost through with life, how near might Ester be to the edge of her own life at that very moment! When the train stopped again, the two were still talking.

"I just hope my boy will look like you," the old lady said suddenly, fixing admiring eyes on the tall, handsome form standing beside her. He had gotten a cup of tea for her and was waiting patiently for her to finish.

Ester followed the glance of her eyes and laughed softly at the extreme improbability of her hope being realized. He answered: "I hope he will be a noble boy and love his mother as she deserves. Then it will matter very little whom he looks like."

While the cup was being returned she smoothed the gray hair back under the plain cap and rearranged and pinned the faded, twisted shawl. Her thoughts seemed troubled suddenly, and she looked up anxiously into the face of her comforter as he again took his seat beside her. "I'm just thinking I'm such a homely old thing, and New York is such a grand place, I've heard them say. I do hope he won't be ashamed of his mother."

"No danger," came the hearty answer. "He'll think you are the most beautiful woman he has seen in ten years."

There is no way to describe the happy look which shone in the faded blue eyes at this response. She laughed softly: "Maybe he'll be like the man I read about the other day. Some mean, old scamp told him how homely his mother was. And he said, says he, 'Yes, she's a homely woman, sure enough; but, oh, she's such a beautiful mother!' Whatever will I do when I get in New York?" she added, with renewed anxiety. "Just as like as not now, he never got a bit of my letter and won't be there to get me!"

"Do you know where your son lives?"

"Oh, yes, I've got it on a piece of paper, the street and the number. But bless your heart, I shouldn't know whether to go up or down or across."

Just the shadow of a troubled look flitted over her friend's face as the thought of the poor old lady, trying to make her way through the city, came to him. He hastened to reassure her. "Then we are all right, whether he meets you or not. We can take a carriage and drive there. I will see you safe at home before I leave you."

This crowning act of kindness brought the tears. "I don't know why you are so good to me," she said simply, "unless you are the friend I prayed for to help me through this journey. If you are, it's all right. God will see that you are paid for it."

And before Ester had finished wondering over the quaintness of this last remark, the engine emitted a triumphant shriek. Then ensued a great din of the most confusing sounds she had ever heard in her life. With everyone hustling and bustling about her, she realized that as soon as they crossed the river on the ferry she would be in New York. Even then she took a curious parting look at the mismatched pair who were winding their way through the crowd and wondered if she would ever see them again.

The next hour was one of utter bewilderment to

Ester. Later she remembered floating across a silver river in a palace and of reaching a place where everybody screamed instead of talked and where all the bells were ringing for fire or something else. She was glad they had arranged for Mr. Newton to take her to her uncle's home. She had not seen her uncle for ten years and would never spot him in a crowd like this. She fumbled for his address in her pocketbook and handed Mr. Newton a recipe for making mince pies instead.

At last, she was whisked along, and carriages, carts and people all seemed to get themselves mysteriously out of the way. She was carried down streets for which the bells must surely be ringing, since they were all ablaze. Ester's escort was to set her down safely at her uncle's door; she had not been able to calculate the precise time of her arrival and was a stranger to her uncle's family, so they had decided upon this easy plan rather than meeting each other at the depot.

Ester was whirled through the streets at a dizzying rate and, with eyes and ears filled with strange sights and sounds, was finally deposited before a beautiful residence, aglow with gas and gleaming with marble. Mr. Newton rang the bell. Ester, amid confused adieus, was ushered into a hall looking not unlike Judge Warren's best parlor back home. Awe mixed with loneliness and almost terror stole over her. The man who had opened the door stood waiting for her response, after a civil "Whom do you wish to see, and what name shall I send up?"

Whom did she wish to see, and what was her name? Could this be her uncle's house? Did she want to see any of them? She half feared them all.

Suddenly the dignity and grandeur melted into gentleness before her, as the tiniest of women appeared, and a cheery, young voice welcomed her heartily: "Is this really my cousin Ester? And so you have come! How perfectly splendid. Where is Mr. Newton? Gone? Why, John, you ought to have smuggled him in to dinner. We are so much obliged to him for taking care of you. John, send those trunks up to my room. You'll room with me, Ester, won't you? Mother thought I ought to put you in a solitary state in a spare chamber, but I couldn't. You see I have been waiting so many years for you that now I want you every bit of the time."

All this while she was giving her loving little pats and kisses on their way upstairs. Such a perfect gem of a room it was into which the traveler was ushered. Ester's love of beauty seemed likely to be gratified fully. In a single glance she took in all the charming details. She then focused upon this wonderful person before her who was the much-dreamed-about, much-longed-for Cousin Abbie in the flesh.

A hundred times Ester had painted her portrait — tall and dark and grand with a regal form and queenly air, hair black as midnight, coiled in heavy masses around her head, eyes blacker if possible than her hair. Sometimes her dress was velvet and diamonds, or, if not the season for it, then a rich, dark silk, but never a material lighter than silk. This had been her picture. She could not suppress a laugh as she noted the contrast between it and the original, for Abbie was two inches shorter than Ester with a manner much more like a fairy's than a queen's. Instead of heavy coils of black hair, little rings of brown curls clustered around a fair, pale forehead and peeped over the bluest of eyes. Her dress was a soft muslin with a pale blue tint. Ester laughed merrily.

"Now have you found something to laugh at in me already?" Abbie asked.

"Why," said Ester, "I'm only laughing to think how totally different you are from your picture."

"From my picture?"

"Yes, the one I'd drawn of you in my mind. I thought you were tall and had black hair and wore silks like a grand lady."

Abbie laughed again. "Don't condemn me to silk in such weather as this. Mother thinks I am barbarous to summon friends to the city in August. But it couldn't very well be avoided. So put on your coolest dress, and be as comfortable as possible."

Ester had been puzzled over how she should dress on this first evening. It would hardly do to put on her blue silk right away. She had meant to choose the black one, but Abbie's laugh and shrug of the shoulder had settled the question of silks. So now she stood confused before her open trunk.

Abbie came to the rescue. "Shall I help you? I won't ring for Nancy tonight but will help you myself. Suppose I hang up some of these dresses? Which one shall I leave out for you? This looks the coolest." She held up the pink and white muslin which served as an afternoon dress at home.

"Well," said Ester with a relieved smile, "I'll wear that," and thought they were not so grand after all.

Presently they went down to dinner. In the splendor of the dining room and the sparkle of glass and the glitter of silver, she changed her mind again and thought them very grand indeed.

Her uncle extended her a very cordial greeting. Ester found it difficult to believe that her Aunt

Helen was three years older than her own mother or that she was a middle-aged lady at all. She was so vivacious and cheerful and altogether unsuitably dressed in Ester's opinion. Yet she thoroughly enjoyed the first two hours of her visit and was surprised and delighted at how easily she slipped into the new ways around her.

Only once was she perplexed: to her great astonishment and dismay she was served a glass of wine. Now Ester was accustomed only to her staunch temperance friends. Her temperance principles, which she assumed were sound and strong, hadn't been tested yet. But here she was at her uncle's table, sitting near her aunt, who was sipping contentedly from her own glass. Would it be proper, under the circumstances, to refuse? Yet would it be proper to violate her sense of what was right?

Ester had no pledge to break, except the pledge with her own conscience. It is sad that that sort of pledge does not seem to be binding in the minds of some people. So Ester toyed with hers and concluded that what her uncle offered for her entertainment must be proper for her to take!

Ester didn't really believe any such thing; she knew she would be judged by her own conscience, not her uncle's. Such an argument simply meant that whatever her uncle offered for her entertainment she hadn't the moral courage to refuse. So she raised the dainty wineglass to her lips and never once thought to look at Abbie and notice how the color mounted and deepened on her face. Nor did she see that her glass remained untouched beside her plate. Ester was frankly glad when the dinner ceremony was ended. Exhausted from her journey, she was excused with Abbie to their room.

CHAPTER IX

Cousin Abbie

ow I have you all to myself," that young lady said with a happy smile, as she turned the key on the retreating Nancy and wheeled an ottoman to Ester's side. "Where shall we begin? I have so much to say and hear. I want to know all about Aunt Laura and Sadie and the twins. Oh, Ester, you have a little brother. Aren't you glad to have one?"

"Why, I don't know," Ester said, hesitating for a moment, then with conviction: "No, I'm always thinking how glad I would be if he were a young man, old enough to escort me places and be company for me."

"I know that's pleasant, but there are serious drawbacks. Now there's our Ralph. It's very pleasant to have him for company. And yet — well, Ester, he isn't a Christian. It seems all the time to me that he is walking on quicksand. I'm constantly afraid for him. I wish so often that he were just a little boy, no older than your brother, Alfred. Then

79

I could learn his tastes and shape them somewhat by having him with me a great deal. I could make religion appear to be such a pleasant thing to him that he couldn't help seeking Jesus for himself. Don't you enjoy teaching Alfred?"

Poor, puzzled Ester! Her cousin asked this question in such a matter-of-fact way. Could she possibly tell her that sometimes she never thought about Alfred from one week's end to another and that she never in her life thought of teaching him a single thing?

"I am not his teacher," she said at length. "I have no time for such things. He goes to school, you know, and Mother helps him."

"Well," said Abbie thoughtfully, "I don't quite mean teaching, either — at least not lessons or the like. I was thinking more of winning him to Jesus. It seems so much easier to do it while one is young. Perhaps he is a Christian now. Is he?"

Ester merely shook her head in answer. She could not look in those earnest blue eyes and say that she had never, by word or act, asked him to come to Jesus.

"Well, that's what I mean. You have so much more chance than I. Oh, my heart is so heavy for Ralph! I am all alone. Ester, do you know that neither my mother nor my father is a Christian, and our home influence is, well, is not what a young man needs. He is very — carefree, you might say. He has friends here in the city and friends in college, but frankly they are not the kind of people I'd like for him to be with. And I'm the only one to stem the tide of worldliness that surrounds him. One thing in particular troubles me — he is, or rather he is not — ," and here poor Abbie stopped. A little silence followed.

After a moment she spoke again: "Oh, Ester, you will learn what I mean without my telling you. I need your help. I depend upon you. I have looked forward to your coming — for his sake as well as for my own. I know it will be better for him."

Ester longed to ask what the "something" was and what was expected of her. But the pained look on Abbie's face deterred her, and she contented herself by saying: "Where is he now?"

"In college — he's coming next week. I long to have a home of my own to show him a better lifestyle than the one he is leading now."

This led to a long talk on the coming wedding.

"Mother is very much disturbed that it should occur in August," Abbie said. "Of course it is not as pleasant as it would be later. But the trouble is, Mr. Foster is obliged to go abroad in September."

"Who is Mr. Foster? Can't you be married if he isn't here?"

"Not very well," Abbie said with a bright little laugh. "You see, he is the one who has asked me to marry him."

"Why, is he?" Ester laughed at her earlier question. Then, as a sudden thought occurred to her, she asked, "Is he a minister?"

"Oh, dear, no, he is only a merchant."

"Is he a — a Christian?" was her next query. She was so unused to conversation on this subject that she actually stammered over the simple sentence.

Such an earnest face turned toward her at this question!

"Ester," said Abbie quickly, "I couldn't marry a man who was not a Christian."

"Why," Ester asked, startled at the energy of her response, "do you think it is wrong?"

"Perhaps not for everyone. I think one's own enlightened conscience should prayerfully decide the question, but it would be wrong for me. I am too weak; it would hinder my own growth in grace. I feel that I need all the human helps I can get. Yes, Mr. Foster is a sincere Christian."

"Do you suppose," asked Ester, "that if Mr. Foster were not a Christian you would marry him?"

A little shiver ran through Abbie's frame as she answered: "I hope I would have strength to do what I thought right, and I believe that would be wrong because the Bible says we should not be unequally yoked. We could not expect to be happy if we went against God's wishes, so I could never do that."

"Yes, you think so now," persisted Ester, "because there is no danger of any such trial. But there are not many Christian young men, Abbie."

Abbie's reply was humble. "Perhaps not, but that would not change me. Ester, *He* has said, 'My grace is sufficient for thee.' "

Then, after a little silence, the sparkle returned to her face as she added: "I am very glad that I am not to be tried in that furnace. I never believed in making myself a martyr to what might have been or even what may be in the future. 'Sufficient unto the day' is my motto. If it should ever be my duty to burn at the stake, I believe I would go to my Savior and plead for sufficient grace. As long as I have no such known trial before me, I don't know why I should ask for what I don't need, or grow unhappy over improbabilities. But I do pray every day to be prepared for whatever the future has for me."

Then the talk drifted back again to the various details connected with the wedding, until suddenly Abbie sprang to her feet.

"Why, Ester!" she exclaimed. "What a thought-less wretch I am! Here I have been chattering at you fairly into midnight, without a thought of your tired body and brain. This session must adjourn immediately. Shall you and I have prayers together tonight? Will it seem homelike to you? Can you play I am Sadie for just a little while?"

"I should like it," Ester answered faintly.

"Shall I read, since you are so weary?" Without waiting for a response, she unclasped the lids of her little Bible. "Are you reading the Bible by a plan? I mean, where do you like best to read for devotions?"

"I didn't know I had a choice." Ester's voice was fainter still.

"Haven't you? I have my special verses that I turn to in my various needs. Where are you and Sadie reading?"

"Nowhere," said Ester desperately.

Abbie's face expressed only innocent surprise.

"Don't you read together? You are roommates, aren't you? Now I always thought it would be so delightful to have a nice little time, like family worship, in one's own room."

"Sadie doesn't care anything about these things. She isn't a Christian," Ester finally admitted.

"Oh, dear! Isn't she?" Abbie spoke in a sad, trou-bled tone. "Then you know something of my anxi-ety, and yet it is different. She is younger than you, and you can have her so much under your influ-ence. At least it seems different to me. How prone we are to consider our own anxieties as especially trying."

Ester had never given a half hour's thought to what was supposed to be such an anxiety to her. But she did not say so, and Abbie continued: "Who is your closest Christian friend then?"

What an exceedingly trying and troublesome talk this was to Ester! What was she to say?

Clearly nothing but the truth.

"Abbie, I haven't a friend in the world."

"You poor, dear child. Then we are in similar situations — though I have dear friends outside of my own family. What a heavy responsibility you must feel in your large household, and you the only Christian. Do you shrink from that kind of responsibility, Ester? Does it seem, sometimes, as if it would almost crush you?"

"Oh, there are some Christians in the family," Ester answered, avoiding the last part of the sentence. "But then — "

"Perhaps they are halfway Christians. I understand how that is. It really seems sadder to me than even thoughtless neglect."

Ester's conscience pricked her. This supposition on Abbie's part was not true. Dr. Van Anden, for instance, always had seemed to her most horribly and fanatically in earnest. But in what rank would she place this young, beautiful, wealthy city lady? Surely she could not be a fanatic?

Ester was troubled.

"Well," said Abbie, "suppose I read you some of my sweet verses. Do you know I always feel a temptation to read in the book of John? There is so much in that book about Jesus, and John seemed to love Him so."

Ester almost laughed. What an exceedingly odd idea — a temptation to read in any part of the Bible. What a strange girl her cousin was.

The reading began. "Here is one of my verses when I am discouraged: 'Wait on the Lord; be of good courage, and he shall strengthen thine heart;

wait, I say, on the Lord!' Isn't that reassuring? And
then these two. Oh, Ester, these are wonderful! 'I
have blotted out, as a thick cloud, thy transgressions, and, as a cloud, thy sins; return unto me; for
I have redeemed thee.' 'Sing, O ye heavens; for the
Lord hath done it; shout, ye lower parts of the
earth; break forth in singing, ye mountains, O for-
est, and every tree therein; for the Lord hath redeemed Jacob, and glorified himself in Israel.' And
in that glorious old prophet's book is my jubilant
verse, 'And the ransomed of the Lord shall return
and come to Zion with songs and everlasting joy
upon their heads; they shall obtain joy and glad-
ness, and sorrow and sighing shall flee away.' "

"Now, Ester, you're very tired, aren't you? I keep
dipping into my treasure like the thoughtless girl I
am. You and I will have some precious readings
out of this book, won't we? Now I'll read you my
sweet good-night psalm. Don't you think the
Psalms are wonderful, Ester?"

And without waiting for a reply the musical
voice read on through that marvel of simplicity
and grandeur, Psalm 121: "'I will lift up mine eyes
unto the hills, from whence cometh my help. My
help cometh from the Lord, which made heaven
and earth. He will not suffer thy foot to be moved:
he that keepeth thee will not slumber. Behold, he
that keepeth Israel shall neither slumber nor sleep.
The Lord is thy keeper: the Lord is thy shade upon
thy right hand. The sun shall not smite thee by
day, nor the moon by night. The Lord shall preserve thee from all evil: he shall preserve thy soul.
The Lord shall preserve thy going out and thy
coming in from this time forth, and even for ever-
more.' "

"Ester, will you pray?" asked her cousin as the

reading ceased, and she closed her tiny book softly.

Ester gave a nervous, hurried shake of her head.

"Then shall I? Or, dear Ester, would you prefer to be alone?"

"No," said Ester, "I should like to hear you." So they knelt, and Abbie's simple, tender prayer Ester carried with her for many a day.

After both heads were resting on their pillows, and quiet reigned in the room, Ester's eyes remained wide open. Abbie had astonished her. She was totally unlike the Cousin Abbie of her dreams and in nothing more so than the strange, childlike, matter-of-fact way in which she talked about religion. Ester had never in her life heard anyone talk like that, except perhaps that minister who had spoken to her in the depot. His religion seemed not unlike Abbie's. Thinking of him, she suddenly addressed Abbie again.

"There was a minister in the depot today, and he spoke to me." Then the entire story of the man with his tract, the girl with blue ribbons, the old lady and the young minister, along with bits of the conversation, was repeated for Abbie's benefit.

Abbie listened and commented and enjoyed every word of it, until the little clock on the mantel spoke in silver tones, one, two. Then Abbie grew penitent again.

"Positively, Ester, I won't speak again. You will be sleepy all day tomorrow, and we will be so busy that you won't even have a chance to wink! Good night."

"Good night," echoed Ester, but she still kept her eyes open. Her journey and her arrival, Abbie and the newness of everything had banished all thoughts of sleep. So she went over in detail everything that had occurred that day. But her thoughts persisted in returning to the question which had so startled her, coming from the lips of a stranger, and to the singleness of heart which seemed to possess her cousin Abbie.

Was she a fellow pilgrim after all? she wondered. If so, what caused the difference between Abbie and her? Only a few hours had passed since she first saw her cousin; yet she distinctly felt the difference between them in that regard. We are as unlike, thought Ester, turning restlessly on her pillow, well, as unlike as any two people can be.

What would Abbie say if she knew that it had, in fact, been months since Ester had read as much in her Bible with any connection as she had heard read that evening? Yes, Ester had gone backward, even as far as that! Farther! What would Abbie say to the fact that she had many, many prayerless days? Not very many perhaps had passed in which she had not used a form of prayer. But there were many in which she had risen from her knees unhelped and unrefreshed, knowing she had not truly prayed a single one of the sentences she had repeated.

Suddenly a thought stunned her — a thought which too often escapes us all. She would not for the world have let Abbie know just how matters stood with her — and yet, and yet Christ knew it all. She lay very still, breathing heavily. This new idea was very disturbing to Ester.

Then that unwearied and ever-watchful Satan came to her aid.

"Oh, well," said he, "your cousin Abbie's surroundings are very different from yours. If you had all the time she has at her disposal, I daresay you would be quite as familiar with your Bible as she is with hers. What does she know about the petty vexations and temptations and constant pressures which harass you every hour of every day? The circumstances are very different. Her life is in the sunshine, yours in the shadow. Besides, you don't know her. It's easy enough to talk and very easy to read a chapter in the Bible. But after all, other things are quite as important, and most likely your cousin is not quite perfect yet."

Ester did not recognize this as a soothing lullaby of the old serpent. It would have been well for her if she had and had answered it with that all-powerful "Get thee behind me, Satan." But she gave her poor brain the benefit of every thought. Having lulled and patted and coaxed her half-roused and startled conscience into quiet rest again, she turned on her pillow and went to sleep.

CHAPTER X

ESTER'S MINISTER

ster was dreaming that the old lady on the train had become an angel and that her voice sounded like a silver bell. She opened her eyes and discovered that it was either the voice of the marble clock on the mantel or the voice of her cousin Abbie, who was bending over her.

"Do you feel able to get up for breakfast, Ester, dear, or would you rather lie here and rest?"

"Breakfast!" echoed Ester, raising herself on one elbow and staring at her cousin.

"Yes, breakfast!" Abbie laughed. "Did you think people in New York lived without such an inconvenience?"

Oh, to be sure, she was in New York, Ester remembered. She laughed too. It had sounded so strange to hear anyone talk to her about getting up for breakfast. It did not seem possible that that meal could be prepared without her help.

"Yes, certainly, I'll get up at once. Have I kept you waiting, Abbie?"

"Oh no, not at all. Generally we breakfast at nine, but Mother gave orders last night to delay until half-past nine this morning."

Ester looked at the little clock in amazement. It was ten minutes to nine! She never recalled sleeping so late in her life before. Why, at home the work in the dining room and kitchen must all be completed by this time, and Sadie was probably making beds. Poor Sadie! What a time she would have! She will learn a little about life while I am away, thought Ester as she stood before the mirror. She pinned the dainty frill on her new pink cambric wrapper, which Sadie's deft fingers had fashioned for her.

Ester had declined Nancy's assistance. She knew better how to get herself ready than she knew how to receive help.

"Now I will leave you for a little," Abbie said, taking up her tiny Bible. "Ester, where is your Bible? I suppose you have it with you?"

Ester looked annoyed. "I don't believe I have," she said quickly. "I packed in such a hurry, you see, that I don't remember putting it in at all."

"Oh, I am sorry — you will miss it so much! Do you have a thousand little private marks in your Bible that nobody else understands? I have a great habit of reading that way. Well, I'll bring you one from the library that you may mark just as much as you please."

Ester sat down beside the open window, holding in her lap the Bible that had just been brought to her. Abbie clearly had left her alone so she could have private devotions. Ester liked the idea very much. To be sure, she hadn't been reading the Bible in the morning. That, she told herself, was because she hardly had time to breathe in the mornings at home. She had beefsteak to cook and breakfast rolls to bake, she thought disdainfully, as if beefsteak and breakfast rolls were the most contemptible items in the world.

She was in a different atmosphere now. At nine o'clock on a summer morning she was dressed in a becoming pink wrapper, finished with the whitest of frills, and sat at her window, a young lady of elegant leisure, waiting for the breakfast bell. Of course, she could read a chapter in the Bible now and would enjoy it quite as much as Abbie did.

She had never learned that happy little habit of having a much-worn, much-loved Bible for her own personal and private use — full of pencil marks and sacred meanings, grown dear from association and teeming with memories of precious inspirations. She had one, of course — a nice, proper-looking Bible — and if it happened to be convenient when she was ready to read, she used it. If not, she picked up Sadie's or Julia's from under the table or the old one on the bookshelf that was missing a cover and part of Revelation; it didn't matter to her which, for there were no pencil marks and no corners of leaves turned down and no special verses to find. She thought the idea of marking certain verses an excellent one and decided to begin doing so at once.

She hunted about for a pencil and found one on the round table by the other window, but many other things were there, too. Abbie's watch lay ticking softly in its marble and velvet bed; she had to examine and sigh over it. Abbie's diamond pin in the jewelry case also demanded attention. Then she had to peep at some blue and gold volumes. Longfellow received more than a peep. Then the most captivating of all lay there, *Say and Seal*, in

two volumes — the very books Sadie had bor-
rowed once and returned before Ester had a chance
to discover how Faith managed about the ring.
Longfellow and the Bible slid down on the table
together, and *Say and Seal* was eagerly seized upon,
just to be glanced at — and the glances continued
until a bell pealed through the house. With a start
and a faint sense of having neglected an opportunity, this Christian young lady followed her cousin
downstairs to meet all the temptations and trials of
a new day. But she would lack the strength she
could have gained through communion with both
her Bible and her Savior.

That breakfast, in all its details, was most fascinating. Ester felt that she could never enjoy that
meal again at a table that was not small and round
and covered with damask. Nor could she drink
coffee that had not first flowed gracefully down
from a silver urn. As for Aunt Helen, she could
have dispensed with her. She even caught herself
drawing unfavorable comparisons between her
and the patient, hardworking mother far away.

"Where is Uncle Ralph?" she asked abruptly, becoming aware that only three were present, when
last evening there had been four.

"He went downtown some hours ago," Abbie
answered. "He is a businessman and cannot keep
such late hours."

"But does he go without breakfast?"

"No — he takes it at seven, instead of nine, like
our lazy selves."

"He used to breakfast at a restaurant downtown,
like other businessmen," explained Aunt Helen
further. "But it is one of Abbie's recent whims to
make him more comfortable at home, so they re-
hearse the interesting scene of breakfast by gas-

light every morning."

Abbie laughed merrily at this. "My dear mother, don't, I beg of you, insult the sun in that manner! Ester, fancy gaslight at seven o'clock on an August morning!"

"Do you get downstairs at seven o'clock?" Ester asked in response.

"Yes, at six or, at most, half-past. If I am to make Father as comfortable at home as he would be at a restaurant, I must flutter around a little."

"She burns her cheeks and fingers over the stove," continued Aunt Helen in a disgusted tone, "so her father may have burnt toast prepared by her hands."

"You've blundered in one item, Mother," was Abbie's good-humored reply. "My toast is never burnt, and only this morning Father pronounced it perfect."

"Oh, she is improving!" her mother answered, with a curious mixture of annoyance and amusement. "If Mr. Foster fails in business soon, as I presume he will, judging from his present rate of progress, she'll be advertising for the position of first-class cook in a small family."

If Abbie felt wounded or vexed over this thrust at Mr. Foster, it showed itself only by a slight deepening of the pink on her cheek, as she answered in the cheeriest of tones: "If I do, Mother, and you engage me, I'll promise you that the eggs will not be boiled as hard as these are."

All this impressed two thoughts on Ester's mind: First, for some reason Ester could not imagine, Abbie of her own free will arose early every morning and prepared breakfast for her father. Second, Abbie's mother said some disagreeable things to her in a disagreeable way — a way that would have provoked Ester and that she would not endure, she said stoutly to herself.

As soon as she and Abbie were alone again, she asked her the first of her questions: "Why do you get breakfast at home for your father, Abbie? Is it necessary?"

"No, only I like it, and he likes it. He has little time to spend at home, and I like that little to be homelike. Besides, Ester, it is my opportunity with my father. I almost never see him alone at any other time, and I am constantly praying that the Spirit will use some small word or act to lead him to the cross."

Ester could make no reply to this, so she turned to the other question: "What did your mother mean by her reference to Mr. Foster?"

"She thinks some of his benevolent schemes are too grand to be prudent. But he is a prudent man and doesn't think so at all."

"Doesn't it annoy you to hear her speak about him in that way?"

The color flushed into Abbie's cheeks again. She hesitated then answered gently: "I think it would, Ester, if she were not my own mother."

Another rebuke. Ester felt irritated anyway. This new, strange cousin of hers was going to prove painfully good.

But her first day in New York, despite the strangeness of everything, thrilled her. They didn't go out, since Ester was supposed to be weary from her journey. In reality she had never felt better. She reveled all day in a sense of freedom — of doing exactly what she pleased or doing nothing. This last experience was so new and strange to her that it was delightful. Ester's round of home duties had pressed so constantly upon her that the rebound was extreme. Right now she hoped she would never have to bake any more pies or cakes in that great oven. She actually shuddered to think that, if she were at home, she would probably be ironing right now, while Maggie did the heavier work.

She fanned herself most vigorously at this thought as she sank back among the luxurious cushions of Abbie's easy chair. She pitied herself and envied Abbie and gave no thought at all to Mother and Sadie, who were working much harder than usual so she could sit here at ease. At last she decided to dismiss every one of these uncomfortable thoughts; to forget that she had ever spent an hour of her life in a miserable, hot kitchen; and to give herself entirely and without reservation to the charmed life, which stretched out before her for three beautiful weeks.

Three weeks is quite a little time, after all, she told herself. Three weeks ago I hadn't the least idea of being here. Who knows what may happen in the next three weeks? Ah! Sure enough, Ester, who knows?

"When am I to see Mr. Foster?" she asked of Abbie as they came up together from the dining room after lunch.

"Why, you will see him tonight, if you are not too tired to go out with me. I was going to ask about that."

"I'm ready for anything; I don't feel as if I ever experienced the meaning of the word *tired*," said Ester briskly, rejoicing at the prospect of going anywhere.

"Well, then, I shall carry you off to our Thursday night prayer meeting. We teachers in the mission — there are fifty of us — have our own meeting. We have the most delightful times. It is like a fam-

ily — rather a large family, perhaps you might
think — but it doesn't seem so when we come on
Sunday from the great congregation and gather in
our dear little chapel. We seem like brothers and
sisters, shutting ourselves in at home to talk and
pray together before we go out into the world
again. Is Thursday your regular prayer meeting
night, Ester?"

Now it would have been difficult for Ester to tell
when her regular prayer meeting night was, since
she had long ago grown out of the habit of attending regularly. She scarcely gave it a thought now.
But she had enough of a conscience left to be
ashamed of this and to know that Abbie referred to
the church prayer meeting. She answered simply,
"No — Wednesday."

"That is our church prayer meeting night. I
missed it last evening because I wanted to welcome you. And Tuesday is our Bible class night."

"Do you give three evenings a week to religious
meetings, Abbie?"

"Yes," said Abbie, "isn't it splendid? I'm grateful
for the privilege, I assure you. So many people
could not do it."

So many people would not, Ester thought.

They did not eat dinner with the family but took
theirs an hour earlier. With David Stewart, a fellow
teacher whom Abbie called her bodyguard, for an
escort, they made their way to Abbie's dear little
chapel, which proved to be a good-sized church,
nicely finished and furnished.

That meeting, from first to last, held a series of
surprises for Ester, beginning with the leader. She
whispered to Abbie: "Your minister is the very
man who spoke to me yesterday in the depot."

Abbie nodded and smiled her surprise at this

information. Ester continued to look about her. In a moment she whispered again: "Why, Abbie, there is the blue-ribboned girl I told you about, sitting in the third seat from the front."

"That," Abbie whispered back, "is Fannie Ames, one of our teachers."

Soon Ester set out to select Mr. Foster from the rows of young men who were rapidly filling the front seats in the left aisle.

I believe that one in glasses is he, she said to herself, regarding him closely. As if to reward her penetration he rose suddenly and came over, book in hand, to the seat directly in front of where they were sitting.

"Good evening, Abbie," came his greeting. "We want to sing this hymn and haven't the tune. Can you lead it without the notes?"

"Why, yes," answered Abbie hesitating. "That is, if you will help me."

"We'll all help," he said, smiling and returning to his seat.

Yes, I'm sure that is he, Ester thought.

Then the meeting began. It was novel. One person, at least, had never attended one just like it. Instead of the chapter of proper length, which Ester thought all ministers selected for public reading, this reader read just three verses. He did not even rise from his seat to do it, nor did he use the pulpit Bible. Instead he read from a bit of a book which he took from his pocket. Then the man in spectacles started a hymn. Ester judged it to be the one without notes from the prompt manner in which Abbie took up the first word.

"Now," said the leader, "before we pray let us have requests." Almost before he had concluded the sentence, a young man responded. "Remember

especially a boy in my class, who seems disposed
to turn every serious word into ridicule."

What a queer subject for prayer, Ester thought.

"Remember my young brother, who seems to be
making the wrong kind of friends," another gentleman said, speaking quickly, as if he realized that he
must hasten or lose his opportunity.

"Pray for everyone in my class. I want them all."
And at this Ester actually started, for the petition
came from the lips of blue-ribboned Fannie Ames
in the corner. A lady actually taking part in a
prayer meeting when gentlemen were present!
How very improper. She glanced around her nervously, but no one else seemed in the least surprised or disturbed. Indeed another young lady
immediately followed her with a similar request.

"Now," said the leader, "let us pray." And that
prayer sounded so strange to Ester. It did not begin
by reminding God that He was the maker and
ruler of the universe or that He was omnipotent
and omnipresent and eternal or by any of the solemn forms of prayer to which her ears were accustomed. It began simply: "Dear Savior, receive these
petitions which we bring. Turn to Yourself the
heart of the lad who ridicules the efforts of his
teacher. Lead the young brother into the straight
and narrow way. Gather that entire class into Your
heart of love." And thus a separate petition for
each separate request was voiced.

As the meeting progressed, it grew more strange
every moment to Ester. Each one seemed to have a
word that he was eager to utter. The prayers, while
very brief, were so pointed as to be almost startling. They sang, too, a great deal, only a verse at a
time and whenever they seemed to feel like it.

Her amazement reached its height when she felt

a little rustle beside her and turned in time to see the eager light in Abbie's eyes as she said: "One of my class has decided for Christ."

"Good news," responded the leader. "Don't let us forget this item of thanksgiving when we pray."

As for Ester she was almost inclined not to believe her ears. Had her cousin Abbie actually "spoken in meeting"? She was about to sink into a reverie over this but hadn't time, for at this moment the leader arose.

"I am sorry," he said, "to cut the thread that binds us, but the hour is gone. Another week will soon pass, though, and, God willing, we shall take up the story. Let's sing." And a soft, sweet chant stole through the room: "Let my prayer be set forth before thee as incense, and the lifting of my hands as evening sacrifice." Then the little company moved with quiet cheer toward the door.

"Have you enjoyed the evening?" Abbie asked eagerly, as they passed down the aisle.

"Why, yes, I believe so; only it was rather odd."

"Odd? Was it? How?"

"Oh, I'll tell you when we get home. Your minister is right behind us, Abbie, and I guess he wants to speak with you."

A bright flush spread over Abbie's face, and a little sparkle danced in her eyes as she turned and gave her hand to the minister. Then she said softly: "Cousin Ester, let me introduce you to my friend, Mr. Edwin Foster."

CHAPTER XI

THE NEW
BOARDER

don't know what to decide," Mrs. Ried said thoughtfully at the pantry door. "Sadie, hadn't I better make these pies?"

"Is that the momentous question you can't decide, Mother?"

Mrs. Ried laughed. "Not quite — it is about the new boarder. We have room enough for another certainly, and seven dollars a week is quite significant now. If Ester were at home, I shouldn't hesitate."

"Mother, if I weren't the meekest and most enduring of mortals, I should be hopelessly frustrated by this time at the constancy with which your thoughts turn to Ester. It is positively insulting, as if I were not doing remarkably. Do you put anything else in apple pies? I never mean to have one, by the way, in my house. I think they're horrid: crust — apples — nutmeg — little lumps of butter all over. Is there anything else, Mother, before I put the top on?"

"Sometimes I sweeten mine a little," her mother answered demurely.

"Oh, sure enough. It was that new boarder that took all thoughts of sweetness out of me. How much sugar, Mother? Do let him come. We are such a stupid family now; it is time we had a new element in it. Besides, you know I broke the largest platter yesterday, and his seven dollars will help buy another. I wish he were anything but a doctor, though. One ingredient of that kind is enough in a family, especially of the variety we have at present."

"Sadie," Mrs. Ried stopped paring the potatoes and looked straight at her daughter. "I never knew a young man for whom I have greater respect than I have for Dr. Van Anden."

"Yes, ma'am," answered Sadie, equally serious. "I have an immense respect for him, I assure you, and so do I for the president. I feel about as intimate with one as the other. I hope Dr. Douglass will be delightfully wild and wicked. How will Dr. Van Anden enjoy the idea of a rival?"

"I spoke of it to him yesterday. I told him we wouldn't give the matter another thought if it would be in any way unpleasant to him. I thought we owed him that consideration in return for all his kindness to us. But he assured me it wouldn't make the slightest difference to him."

"Do let him come, then. I believe I need another bed to make. I'm growing thin for want of exercise, and, by the way, that suggests a mark in his favor. As a doctor, he will be out all night sometimes perhaps, and the bed won't need making so often. Mother, I do believe I didn't put a speck of soda in that cake I made this morning. What will that do to it? Or rather, what will it not do, since it is not there

to do it? As for Ester, I shall consider it a personal
insult if you mention her again, when I am filling
her place so magnificently."

The patient mother laughed and groaned at almost the same time. Poor Ester never forgot the
soda or anything else. But Sadie was so merry and
full of good humor.

Finally it was decided; the new boarder came
and was duly initiated into the family. Thus began
a new era in Sadie's life. Lighthearted clerks and
schoolboys she counted among her acquaintances
by the score. Grave, dignified, slightly taciturn
men of the Dr. Philip Van Anden stamp she num-
bered also among her friends, but never one quite
like Dr. Stephen Douglass. This easy-going, courteous gentleman seemed always to say or do just the
right thing at the right moment. He was dressed in
the latest styles which enhanced his refined fea-
tures. He was neither wild nor sober, seemed the
furthest thing possible from wicked, yet was never
in any way disagreeably good.

His relationship with Sadie progressed rapidly.
A new element had entered her life. The golden
days when the two sisters had been together often,
when the Christian sister might have planted seed
for the Master in Sadie's bright young heart, had
gone. Perhaps that sleeping Christian, Ester, who
was nestled so cozily among the cushions in
Cousin Abbie's morning room, might have been
startled and aroused, if she had realized those days
would never return. Misspent they had passed
away. A new worker had come to drop seed into
the unoccupied heart. Never again would Sadie be
as fresh and innocent or as easily won as in those
days she had let slip by in idle, aye, worse than
idle, slumber.

Sadie sealed and addressed a letter to Ester and hastened downstairs with it. Dr. Douglass stood at the doorway, hat in hand.

"Shall I have the pleasure of being your carrier?" he asked.

"Are you to be trusted?" Sadie questioned, as she quietly deposited the letter in his hat.

"That depends in a great measure on whether you trust me. The world is safer in general than we are inclined to think it. Who lives in that little bird's nest of a cottage just across the way?"

"A dear old gentleman, Mr. Vane," Sadie answered, her voice softening as it always did whenever she was reminded of Florence. "That's he standing in the gateway. Doesn't he look like a grand old patriarch?"

As they were watching Mr. Vane, Dr. Van Anden's carriage turned the corner suddenly. He reined in his horses in front of the opposite gateway. They could hear his words distinctly.

"Mr. Vane, let me advise you to avoid this evening breeze. It is blowing up strongly from the river."

"Is Dr. Van Anden the old gentleman's nurse or guardian or what?" ventured Sadie's companion.

"Physician" was her brief reply. After a moment she laughed mischievously. "You don't like Dr. Van Anden, do you?"

"I? Oh, yes, I like him. The trouble is, he doesn't like me. He isn't to blame, to be sure. Probably he cannot help it. I have in some way succeeded in offending him. Why do you think I am not one of his admirers?"

"Oh," answered this rude, uninhibited girl, "I thought it would be very natural for you to be slightly jealous of him, professionally, you know."

If her object was to embarrass or annoy Dr. Douglass, she apparently did not achieve it. He chuckled: "Professionally he is to be envied. I regard him as a very skillful physician, Miss Ried."

Before Sadie could reply, the horses were stopped at the door, and Dr. Van Anden called to her: "Sadie, do you want to take a ride?"

Sadie had no special fondness for Dr. Van Anden, but she loved his horses and cultivated their acquaintance at every opportunity. Five minutes later she was skimming over the road with the wind buoying her spirits. Afterward Sadie recalled that night as the last one in which she rode behind those black ponies for some time.

The doctor seemed more relaxed than usual and in a much more talkative mood. It was quite a merry ride, until he broke a moment of silence by an abrupt question: "Sadie, haven't your mother and you always considered me a sincere friend to your family?"

Sadie's reply was prompt and to the point. "Certainly, Dr. Van Anden, I have as much respect for and confidence in you as I would have had for my grandfather, if I'd ever known him."

"That being the case," continued the doctor, "you will give me credit for sincerity and honesty in what I am about to say. I want to warn you about Dr. Douglass. He is not a man I can respect, nor is he a man with whom I would like to see my sister being so friendly. I have known him well and for a long time, Sadie."

Sadie Ried never fretted or became petulant, and rarely was she angry. But when she was, it was a genuine case of unrestrained rage. Woe to the individual who fell victim to her blazing eyes and caustic tongue. Tonight Dr. Van Anden was that

victim. What right had he to arraign her before him
and say with whom she should or should not asso-
ciate, as if he were indeed her very grandfather?
What business had he to think that she was too
friendly with Dr. Douglass?

With the usual blindness that belongs to angry
people, it had not once occurred to her that Dr. Van
Anden had said and done none of these things.
When she felt she could keep her voice steady, she
spoke: "You are very kind, Dr. Van Anden, extremely so. I am happy to reassure you, though,
that as yet I feel myself in no danger from Dr.
Douglass's fascinations, however remarkable they
may be. My mother and I enjoy excellent health at
present, so you don't need to worry about our
choice of physicians. Of course it's natural for you
to feel nervous, I guess. But you will pardon me for
saying that I consider your interference with my
affairs unnecessary and uncalled for."

If Dr. Van Anden wanted to reply to this insulting harangue, he had no opportunity, for just then
they whirled around the corner and arrived at
home.

Sadie rushed inside and threw down her hat.
Seating herself at the piano, she literally stormed
the keys. The doctor stepped back into his carriage
and set out quietly to make his evening round of
calls.

What a whirlwind of rage stewed in Sadie's
heart! What earthly right had this detestable man
to give her advice? Was she a child to be ordered
about by anyone? What right had anyone to speak
in that way of Dr. Douglass? He was a gentleman,
certainly, much more so than Dr. Van Anden had
shown himself to be — and she liked him. Yes, and
she would like him, in spite of a whole corps of

106   ISABELLA MACDONALD ALDEN

Sadie heard a light step cross the hall and enter
the parlor. She raised her eyes long enough to be
certain that it was Dr. Douglass who stood beside
her, and then she continued her playing.

He leaned over the piano and listened. "Did you
have a pleasant ride?" he asked during a brief lull
in the music.

"Charming."

"I judged by the pace of the music that there
must have been a hurricane."

"Nothing of the sort. Only a little paternal advice."

"Indeed! Have you been taken into his kindly
care? I congratulate you."

Sadie was still very angry. It is lamentable that
people will say and do strange things when they
are angry — things they repent of in cooler moments. Fixing her eyes on Dr. Douglass, she said
abruptly: "He was warning me against the impropriety of associating with your dangerous self."

A pained expression crossed the doctor's face.
More to himself but aloud he said: "Is that man
determined I shall have no friends?"

Touched, Sadie struck soft, sweet chords on the
piano: "What is your offense in his eyes, Dr.
Douglass?"

Dr. Douglass stammered a reply. "Why — I —
he — I would rather not tell you, Miss Ried. It
sounds bad." Then with a sad laugh he continued,
"And that half admission sounds bad, too — worse
than the simple truth, perhaps. Well, I had the mis-
fortune to cross his path professionally once — a
slight mistake that is not worth repeating. Neither
would I repeat it if it were in honor to him. He is a
skillful man and since then has become prominent.

I can't imagine that he would still remember that incident now, but it seems as if he has never forgiven me."

The music ceased, and Sadie's great honest eyes were fixed in horror on his face. "Can that be all," she said at length, "for him to bear such ill-will toward you? And they call him an earnest Christian!"

Dr. Douglass could not restrain a laugh at that remark. Then he became instantly serious. "I beg your pardon."

"For what, Dr. Douglass? Why did you laugh?"

"For laughing. And I laughed because I could not keep from being amused at your connection of his unpleasant state of mind with his professions of Christianity."

"Shouldn't they be connected?"

"Well, that depends upon how much importance you attach to them."

"Dr. Douglass, what do you mean?"

"Treason, I suspect, viewed from your standpoint. Therefore it would be much more proper for me not to talk about it."

"But I want you to talk about it. Do you mean to say that you have no faith in anyone's religion?"

"How much have you?"

"Dr. Douglass, that is a very Yankee way of answering a question."

"I know, but it is the easiest way of reaching my point. I repeat: How much faith do you have in these Christian professions? In other words, how many professing Christians do you know who are, in your opinion, improved by their professions?"

The questions that had plagued Sadie's own heart were brought before her again! Oh, Christian sister, with whom she had spent so many years, with whom she had been so closely connected! If she could only have turned to you and remembered your earnest life, your honest endeavors toward the right, your earnest struggles with sin and self, she would have seen evidence of the Lord Jesus all about you. She could then have quelled the tempter in human form, who stood waiting for a verdict. She could have declared: "I have known one." What might not have been gained for your side that night?

CHAPTER XII

THREE PEOPLE

s it was, she hesitated and thought not of Ester, whose life had not amounted to much of consequence, but of her mother.

Mrs. Ried's religion had in truth been more negative than positive, at least outwardly. She never spoke much of these matters, and Sadie did not know for certain if she ever prayed. So how could she decide whether the gentle, patient life was the outgrowth of religion in her heart, or whether it was a naturally sweet disposition?

Then there was Dr. Van Anden; an hour ago she would surely have named him, but now it was impossible. The silence increased, as well as the peculiar smile on Dr. Douglass's face, and so did Sadie's discomfort until she answered hurriedly: "I don't know many Christian people, doctor. But I don't consider those to be in any way remarkable. At the same time I don't choose to set down the entire Christian world as miserable hypocrites."

"Not at all," the doctor answered quickly. "I have many friends whom I respect very highly among that class of people. But since you have pressed me to continue this conversation, I must confess that my esteem is not based on the fact that they are called Christians. I — but, Miss Ried, this is entirely unlike me to shake your innocent, trusting faith. I wouldn't do it for the world."

Sadie interrupted him impatiently. "Don't talk nonsense, Dr. Douglass, if you can help it. I don't feel innocent at all, just now at least, and I have no particular faith to shake. If I had I hope you wouldn't think it so flimsy as to be shaken by anything you have said thus far. I certainly have heard no arguments. Sometimes I think about things. I must admit I have been a little puzzled to notice the inconsistency that exists between the profession and the practice of these people. If you have any explanation, I'd like to hear it."

"I have offered no arguments, nor do I mean to," Dr. Douglass cautioned. "I was apologizing for having touched upon this matter at all. I'm unfortunate in my belief, or rather disbelief. But I have no intention of forcing it upon others. I do believe there are some very good, nice, pleasant people in the world. Whether through the accidents of birth or education, they have been taught to believe that they are aided in being good by something more than human power. This belief helps them to mature into naturally sweet, pure individuals. I explain their apparent inconsistencies by the idea that they have never realized the full moral force of the rules they profess to follow. I divide the world, the so-called Christian world, into two distinct classes. Those I've just named constitute one class, and the other is made up of unmitigated hypocrites. Now, my friend, I have talked longer on this subject than I like, or than I ought to have. I beg you to forget all I have said and play some music to end the evening."

Sadie laughed and ran her fingers lightly over the keys. "In which class do you place your brother in the profession, doctor?"

Dr. Douglass shrugged his shoulder very slightly. "It is proper, and also rare, for a physician to be eminent not only for skill but piety. My fellow practitioner is a wise and wary man, who —." He stopped himself from going further.

"Miss Ried," he added after a moment, in a different tone, "which of us is at fault tonight, you or I, that I seem bent on making uncharitable remarks? I really did not imagine myself to be so totally depraved. To be honest, I'm very sorry this conversation started. I didn't intend it. I don't believe in interfering with the beliefs or changing the opinions of others."

Sadie had apparently recovered her good humor, for her laugh was again as light and carefree as usual. "Don't distress yourself unnecessarily, Dr. Douglass. You haven't harmed me in the least. I don't believe a word you say, and furthermore I don't think you believe more than two-thirds of it yourself. Now I'm going to play you the stormiest piece of music you ever heard in your life." And the keys rattled and rang under her touch and beckoned half a dozen loungers from the halls to the parlor, ending the conversation.

That night three people in the household held a conversation with their own thoughts. To finite eyes those conversations would have wonderfully benefitted the right if the three had assembled and spoken together, instead of in the quiet and privacy of their own rooms.

Sadie had calmed down and was naturally ashamed of herself. As she rolled up, pinned and otherwise snuggled her curls into order for the night, she scolded herself: "Sadie Ried, you made a simpleton of yourself in that speech to Dr. Van Anden tonight. Just because you think a man interferes with what doesn't concern him is no reason to grow flushed and angry and forget that you're a lady. You said some very rude and insulting words. You know your dear mother would tell you so if she knew anything about it, which she won't — that's one comfort. Besides you have probably offended those delightful black ponies. It will be forever before they take you for another ride, and that's worse than all the rest. But who would think of Dr. Van Anden being such a man?

"I wish Dr. Douglass had gone to Europe before he told me; it was rather pleasant to believe in the extreme goodness of somebody. I wonder how much of that nonsense Dr. Douglass believes, anyway? Perhaps he is half right. But I'm not going to think any such thing, because it would be wicked, and I'm good. And because" — gently caressing an old worn book which lay on her bureau — "this is my father's Bible, and he lived and died by its precepts."

Up another flight of stairs in his own room, Dr. Douglass lit a cigar, settled in his armchair with his feet on the dressing table and, between puffs, commiserated: "I'm sorry we ran into this miserable train of talk tonight, but that young charmer leads a man on so. I'm glad she has a decided mind of her own; one feels less guilty. I'm what they call a skeptic myself, but I don't like to see a lady become one. I won't lead her astray. I wouldn't have said anything tonight if it hadn't been for that miserable hypocrite of a Van Anden. The fellow must learn not to pitch into me if he wants to be left alone. I doubt if he gained much this time. What a charmer she is!" Dr. Douglass removed his cigar long enough to let out a hearty laugh in recalling some of Sadie's remarks.

Just across the hall Dr. Van Anden sat at his table, one hand partly shading his eyes from the light while he read. "O let not the oppressed return ashamed: let the poor and needy praise thy name. Arise, O God, plead thine own cause: remember how the foolish man reproacheth thee daily. Forget not the voice of thine enemies; the tumult of those that rise up against thee increaseth continually."

Something troubled the doctor tonight; his usually serious face was marked with sadness. Presently he arose and paced slowly up and down the room.

"I ought to have done it," he said at last. "I ought to have told her mother that he was an unsafe companion for Sadie, especially in this. He is a sly, fascinating skeptic — all the more fascinating because he will be careful not to shock her with any bold lies. I should have warned them. Why did I shrink so miserably from my duty! What did it matter if they ascribed a wrong motive to my concern? It was still my duty." The sad lines deepened on his face as he marched slowly back and forth. But he was nearer a solution to his problems than the other two were. At last he returned to his chair and sank before it on his knees.

Now all three, in their own separate ways, were mistaken. Sadie had said she would not believe the nonsense Dr. Douglass spoke; she honestly imagined that she was not influenced in the least. And yet, the poison had entered her soul. As the days passed, she found herself objecting more and more to the weaknesses of those who professed to be Christians. She was quick to detect their mistakes and failures and far more willing to admit that the entire subject might be a cunningly devised tale.

Sadie was the child of many prayers, and her father's Bible with its worn edges lay on her dressing table; it continued to speak for him, now that his tongue was silent in the grave. As a result she did not quite yield to the enemy, though she was certainly tiptoeing near the door of temptation. The Christian tongues around her, which the grave had not silenced, remained as mute as though their lips were already sealed. Thus the path Sadie tread grew daily broader and more dangerous.

Then there was Dr. Douglass: he was not by any means the worst man in the world. He was, or fancied himself to be, a skeptic. Like many his age who are wise in their own conceits, he had no distinct idea of what he was skeptical about, nor did he fancy to what heights of illogical nonsense his views, if carried out, would lead him. Like many others, he had studied rhetoric, logic, mathematics and medicine thoroughly. He would have hesitated and studied and pondered long before disputing an established point in surgery. Yet, in accord with the folly of the age, he had decided upon the errancy of the Bible after giving it, at most, only a careless reading here and there. Nor had he ever once sincerely used the means by which God has promised to enlighten those who seek after knowledge. Blinded, he did not realize how absurd and unreasonable and utterly foolish was his conduct.

Be that as it may, Dr. Douglass sincerely intended to do Sadie no harm. But, as the days came and went, he was continually harming her. They were often in each other's company, and that subject which he meant to avoid was constantly intruding. Both were so alert to see and hear the unwise, inconsistent and unchristian acts and words, for, alas, there were so many to be seen and heard, that these two made rapid strides on the broad road.

Finally, there was Dr. Van Anden, who carried a sad, heavy heart. He felt that he had shrunk from his duty, hiding behind that most miserable of all excuses: What will people think? If Douglass had had any title other than doctor prefixed to his name, he would immediately have advised Mrs. Ried about him. But how could he endure their suspecting that he was jealous of Douglass? In trying to right the wrong — by warning Sadie — he realized, as many a poor Christian has before and after him, that he was making the sacrifice too late and in vain.

There was one other thing: Dr. Douglass's statements to Sadie had been colored with truth. Among his other honest mistakes was the belief that Dr. Van Anden was a hypocrite. They had clashed in former years. Dr. Douglass had been more in the wrong, though what man, without the help of Christ, was ever known to believe this of himself? But there had been wrong on the other side, too. Hasty words were spoken — words which rankled then, and rankled still, after the lapse of years. Dr. Van Anden had never said: I should not have spoken thus; I am sorry. He had taught himself to believe that it would be an unnecessary humiliation for him to say this to a man who had so deeply wronged him!

But, to do our doctor justice, time had healed the wound in him. Personal enmity had not prompted his warning, nor did he have any inkling of the injury his sharp words were causing in the unsanctified heart. When he dropped upon his knees that night he prayed earnestly for the conversion of Sadie and Dr. Douglass.

So these three lived under that same roof and did not guess what the end might be.

CHAPTER XIII

THE STRANGE CHRISTIAN

bbie," said Ester, wriggling around from before the open trunk in the center of their room. A mass of collars and cuffs slid onto the rich-hued carpet. "Do you know that I think you're the strangest girl I ever knew in my life?"

"I'm sure I didn't," Abbie answered cheerfully. "If it's a nice 'strange,' do tell me about it. I'd like to be nice — ever so much."

"Well, but I am sincere, Abbie. You truly are. These collars made me think of it. Oh, dear me! They are all on the floor." She reached after the shiny, sliding things.

Abbie sat down on the green velvet rocker beside her, holding a mass of puffy lace which she was straightening out.

"Suppose we have a little talk," she said. "Please tell me, Ester, plainly and simply, what you mean by the term *strange*. I have heard it so often that sometimes I fear I really am painfully unlike other people. You are just the one to enlighten me."

117

Ester laughed a little. "You're taking the matter too seriously. I didn't mean anything dreadful."

"Ah, but you are not to be excused in that way, my dear Ester. Mother has made the same remark many times, but it's usually connected with religious topics. Mother, you know, is not a Christian, so I've thought that perhaps some things seemed strange to her which would not to — you, for instance. But ever since your arrival you've mentioned your surprise about me several times and showed it on your face even more often. Today even my stiff and glossy and, in every way, proper collars and cuffs arouse it. Do please tell me, should I be in an asylum somewhere instead of preparing to go to Europe?"

Ester laughed again at the mixture of comedy and pathos in Abbie's voice, yet something in the words embarrassed her. She struggled with her thoughts, then spoke honestly. "Well, the strangeness is connected with religious topics in my mind also. Even though I profess to be a Christian, I do not understand you. I am conservative in my dress, you know, Abbie. I don't care for these things in the least. But if I had the money as you have, I would have a great many things. Your economy makes no earthly sense in your financial situation; yet you hesitate over expenses almost as much as I do."

Mischief twinkled in Abbie's eyes. "Will you tell me, Ester, why you would take the trouble to get 'these things' if you do not care for them in the least?"

"Why, because — because they would be proper and befitting of my station in life."

"Do I dress in a manner unbecoming to my station in life?"

"No," said Ester promptly, admiring the crimson finishings of her cousin's morning robe. "But then — well, Abbie, do you think it is wicked to like nice things?"

"No," Abbie answered very gently, "but I think it is wrong to school ourselves into believing that we do not care for anything of the kind, when in reality it is a higher, purer motive which deters us from having many things. Forgive me, Ester, but I think you are unjust sometimes to your better self in this way."

Ester gave a little start and realized for the first time in her life that, though she loved truth, she had been practicing a pretty little deception of this kind by pretending not to care for frills and laces. In a moment, however, she returned to the charge.

"But, Abbie, did Aunt Helen really want you to have that pearl velvet we saw at Stewart's?"

"She really did."

"And you refused it?"

"And I refused it."

"Well, is that to be pawned off on religion, too?" she asked in her old, familiar sharp tone.

Abbie's eyes reflected her surprise. "I think we don't understand each other," she finally said quietly. "That dress, Ester, with all its accessories could not have cost less than seven hundred dollars. Could I, a follower of the meek and lowly Jesus, living in a world where so many of His poor are suffering, have worn such a dress as that? My dear, I see now how these pretty little collars — and by the way, Ester, you are crushing one of them against that green box — suggested the thought. But you surely do not consider it strange, when I have so many collars already, that I didn't pay thirty dollars for that bit of a cobweb we saw yesterday?"

"But Aunt Helen wanted you to."

A sad look stole over Abbie's face. "My mother, remember, dear Ester, does not realize that she is not her own but has been bought with a price. You and I know that we must give an account of our stewardship. Ester, do you see how people who ask God to help them in every little decision — in the least expenditure of money — can, after that, deliberately fritter it away?"

"Do you ask God's help in these matters?"

"Why, certainly," Abbie said, with a look of wonder again — an expression Ester had learned to know and dislike. " 'Whatsoever therefore ye do' — you know."

"But, Abbie, going out shopping to buy — handkerchiefs, for instance — that seems to me a very small thing to pray about."

"Even the purchase of handkerchiefs may involve a question of conscience, Ester. I think you would agree if you were to see the box that hasn't a bit of air for all the puffs of handkerchiefs filling it. Somehow I can never feel that any detail in my life is of less importance than a tiny sparrow, and yet He looks after them."

"Abbie, do you mean to say that in every little thing you buy you weigh the subject and discuss the right and wrong of it?"

"I do try to find out just what is right and then do it. No act in this world is so small as to be neither right nor wrong."

"Then," said Ester, with an impatient twitch of her dress from under Abbie's rocker, "I don't see the use of being rich."

"Nobody is rich, Ester, only God. But I'm so glad sometimes that He has trusted me with a small portion of His wealth that I feel like praying a prayer of thanksgiving about that one thing. What else am I strange about, Ester?"

"Everything," she said with growing impatience. "I think it was very odd in you not to go to the concert last evening with Uncle Ralph."

"But, Ester, it was prayer meeting night."

"Well, so what? Prayer meeting convenes every week. This particular singer doesn't perform very often, and Uncle Ralph was disappointed. I thought you believed in honoring your parents."

"You forget, Ester, that Father said he was particularly eager for me to do as I thought right and that he would not have purchased the tickets if he had remembered the meeting. Father likes consistency."

"Well, that is just the point. Do you call it inconsistent to leave your prayer meeting for just one evening, no matter for what reason?"

Abbie laughed and shook her brown curls. "I don't think you would make a good lawyer, Ester. You don't stick to the point." She added more seriously, "I try to be very careful in this matter too. The city has so many activities, that unless I draw the line firmly I wouldn't get to prayer meeting at all. On some occasions, of course, I must be occupied elsewhere, but under ordinary circumstances it must be more than a concert that occupies me."

"I don't believe in making religion such a solemn matter as all that sounds. It has a tendency to drive people away from it."

Abbie's face, in response to this rather contentious remark, betrayed a mixture of bewilderment and pain. She kept some of her thoughts to herself. But at length she said, "I don't understand. How is that a solemn matter? If we really expect to meet our Savior at a prayer meeting, isn't it a delightful thought? I'm very happy when I can go to the place of prayer."

Ester sounded exactly as she did in her worst moods in that long dining room at home.

"Of course, I should have remembered that Mr. Foster would be at the prayer meeting and not at the concert. That was reason enough for your enjoyment."

Abbie's face grew red during this rude address, but she did not utter a single word. When next she spoke, it was with a voice that trembled with emotion.

"Ester, one thought troubles me very much. Do you really think, as you have intimated, that I am selfish, that I consider my own desires too much, and so injure the cause? For instance, do you think I prejudiced my father?"

What a sweet, humble, even tearful, face she had! And what a question to ask Ester! What had caused Ester's disagreeable state of mind except the struggles of her hitherto quiet conscience over the contrast between Cousin Abbie's life and her own.

Here in the face of her theories to the contrary, in defiance of her belief in the decadent life-style that prevailed in the city, in the heart of this great city, and in the midst of wealth and temptations, Ester had found this young lady, daughter of one of the merchant princes. Abbie moved sweetly, brightly, quietly through the elaborate wedding plans, and yet evidently she found her greatest pleasure in the presence of her Savior.

All of Ester's speculations about Abbie had come to naught. She had planned the wardrobe of the bride over and over again for days before she saw her. While she had prepared proper little lectures for her on the folly of fashionable attire, she had still delighted in the beauty and elegance around her. How her ideals had been thwarted! Beauty there certainly was in everything, but it was the beauty of simplicity, not at all of silks and velvets and jewels as Ester had imagined.

It certainly could not be wealth that made Abbie's life such a happy one, for she regulated her expenses with such care and forethought that Ester had never dreamed of. It could not be a life of ease or freedom from annoyance that kept her bright and sparkling; it had taken only a week's sojourn in her aunt's home for Ester to discover that all wealthy people were not amiable and delightful. Abbie was evidently stretched and rubbed in a hundred little ways, having a hundred little trials which she herself had never been called upon to endure.

In short, Ester had discovered that merely living in a great city was not in itself calculated to make running the Christian race any easier or more pleasant. She had even begun to suspect that it might not be as easy as it was in a quiet country home. One by one all her explanations of Abbie's peculiar character had popped like bubbles. What then sustained and guided her cousin? Ester could draw only one conclusion: It was simply constant, thorough Christian faith and trust. But then didn't she have this same faith? Yet could any contrast be greater than that of Abbie's life with hers?

Ester's conscience was being challenged as never before. Her conscience had been in a new atmosphere for one whole week, and it was roused. It was not fully awake yet, but restless and on the alert — and it would not be hushed back into its lethargic state!

This was why Ester was such an uncomfortable companion this morning. She was not willing to be shaken and roused. Her words to Abbie had been unkind and rude. And instead of throwing an uncontrollable fit which Ester expected, Abbie sat still, meekly and humbly awaiting her verdict. How Ester wished she had never asked that last question! How ridiculous she would appear, after all that had been said, if she admitted that her cousin's life had been one continual reproach of her own. On the very matter of the concert, she had heard Uncle Ralph say that if all the world matched what they did with what they said as well as Abbie did, he might be a Christian himself. Then what if Ester added that this very direct remark had been made to her when she was accompanying her uncle and aunt to that same concert.

Ester was disgusted and wished she could start the conversation over. She felt certain now that she would leave a great many things unsaid. The unrest and dissatisfaction in her heart was showing in her countenance.

Abbie started to speak, but she was interrupted by a loud banging on the front door downstairs. Then the sound of hurried footsteps and an unfamiliar voice in the hall floated up to Ester. Abbie flung down her thimble and scissors. "Ralph has come!" she exclaimed and disappeared.

CHAPTER XIV

THE LITTLE CARD

eft to herself, Ester found her train of thought so disagreeable that she hastened to get rid of it and seized upon the newcomer to afford her a substitute.

This cousin, whom she was expected to influence for good, had at last arrived. Ester had had a strong interest in him ever since that evening of her arrival, when his sister had appealed to her to use her influence on him — just how she hadn't any idea. Abbie had never spoken of it since and seemed to have lost her desire for the cousins to meet. Ester mused about all this now; she wished she knew how she was to help.

Abbie was evidently troubled about him. Perhaps he was rough and awkward; schoolboys often were, even those born in a city. Ralph had spent most of his life away from home. She had heard that boys away from the atmosphere and training at home were inclined to become rude and coarse. He was shy, too, of course; he was about the age to

125

be that. He must feel out of place in the grand mansion which he called home but where he had passed so little time. She could imagine just how he looked. He probably didn't know what to do with his hands or his feet, and most likely he sat on the edge of his chair and ate with his knife. School was a horrid place for picking up all sorts of bad manners. All these things must annoy Abbie very much, especially now when he must come in contact with that perfection of gentlemanliness, Mr. Edwin Foster. I wish, thought Ester anxiously, I wish we had more than a week before the wedding. But I'll do my best. Abbie shall see I'm good for something. Although I do differ with her somewhat in her peculiar views, I believe I know how to conduct myself in almost any situation — even if I have been brought up in the country.

By the time the lunch bell rang, a girl more satisfied with herself and her benevolent intentions than Ester could hardly have been found. She stood in front of the mirror smoothing out the silken bands of brown hair before tying a blue satin ribbon over them when Abbie returned.

"Forgive me many times over for rushing off as I did and leaving you behind and then staying away so long. I haven't seen Ralph in such a long time that I forgot everything else. Your hair doesn't need another bit of brushing, Ester — it's as smooth as velvet. They're all waiting for us in the dining room, and I want to show you to Ralph." And before the blue satin ribbon was tied quite to her satisfaction, Ester was hurried to the dining room to assume her new role of guide and general assistant to the awkward youth.

I suppose he hasn't any idea what to say to me, was her last compassionate thought, as Abbie's hand rested on the knob. I hope he won't be hopelessly quiet, but I'll manage in some way.

At first he was nowhere to be seen. Abbie said eagerly, "Ralph, here is Cousin Ester!"

The door swung back into its place and revealed a tall, well-proportioned young man with a full-bearded face and dancing eyes. He came forward immediately, extending both hands and speaking rapidly. "Long-hoped-for come at last! I don't refer to myself, you understand, but to this eagerly anticipated prospect of greeting my cousin Ester. Should I welcome you, or you me — which is it? I'm somewhat confused as to proprieties. Getting this close to a wedding has muddled my brain. Sis" — turning suddenly to Abbie — "have you prepared Ester for her fate? Does she understand that she and I are to officiate — that is, if we don't evaporate before the eventful day? Sis, how could your conscience let you carry out a wedding in August? Whatever takes Foster abroad just now, anyway?" And without waiting for answers to his unending questions he rambled cheerily on.

Clearly whatever his shortcomings might be, inability to talk was not one of them. And Ester, bewildered and utterly thrown off course, was more silent and awkward than she had ever known herself to be. She was provoked, too, with Abbie, with Ralph, with herself.

How could I have been such a simpleton? she wondered. Seated opposite her cousin at the table, she had an opportunity to study his handsome face with its changes in expression. She noted the pleased attention even her uncle paid to his ceaseless flow of words.

Ester's thoughts flowed through her mind as ceaselessly as his words. I knew he was older than

Abbie and that this was his third year in college. What could I have expected from Uncle Ralph's son? He must think I'm a dunce, blushing and stammering like an awkward country girl. What on earth could Abbie mean about being troubled about him and needing me to help him? It is some of her ridiculous fanatical nonsense, I suppose. I wish she talked and acted like everybody else.

"But I don't know that that's the case," Ralph was saying, when Ester returned from her own thoughts. "I can simply guess at it, which is as close to exertion as a fellow ought to be forced to make in this weather. John, you may fill my glass, if you please. Father, this is even better wine than your cellar usually affords, and that is saying a great deal. Sis, has Foster made a temperance woman of you entirely? I see you are devoted to ice water."

"Oh, certainly," Aunt Helen answered for her, in the half-contemptuous tone she assumed on such occasions. "I warn you, Ralph, to get all the enjoyment you can out of the present, for Abbie intends to keep you with her entirely after she has a home of her own — out of the reach of temptation."

Ester glanced at her cousin. How did her aunt find out Abbie's pet scheme? And how could Abbie possibly maintain her self-control under the ridicule which was so apparent in her mother's voice?

The pink on her cheek deepened noticeably, but she answered with perfect good humor: "Ralph, don't be frightened, please. I shall let you out once in a long while if you are very good."

Ralph bent loving eyes on the sweet, young face. "I don't know that I shall care for even that reprieve, since you're to be jailer."

What could be in this young man to cause anxiety? What needed to be changed? Yet even while Ester puzzled, he passed his glass for a third filling. Ester saw Abbie's quick, pained look, then her downcast eyes and deeply flushing face. She knew at once that the mischief lay in that wine glass. Abbie thought him to be in danger. This was the meaning of her unfinished sentence on that first evening and her embarrassed silence since; for Ester, with her filled glass always beside her plate, sometimes untouched but more often sipped from in response to her uncle's invitation, was not the one from whom help could be expected in this. Ester wondered if the handsome face opposite her could be in real danger, or was this another of Abbie's whims? At least it wasn't pleasant to be drinking wine before him. She left her glass untouched that day and felt troubled about that and everything.

The next morning they went on a shopping excursion, and Ralph was smuggled in as an attendant. Abbie fingered through the endless sets of handkerchiefs in a quandary.

"Take this box — do, Abbie," Ester urged. "This monogram in the corner is lovely, and that is the dearest little sprig of flowers in the world."

"Which is precisely what troubles me," laughed Abbie. "It is entirely too dear. Think of paying such an enormous sum for handkerchiefs!"

Ralph, who was resting near her and trying not to look bored, raised his eyebrows at the remarks. He whispered to her: "Is Foster hard up? If he is, you are not on his hands yet, Sis. And I think Father is good for all the finery you may happen to fancy."

"That only shows your ignorance of the subject.

I fear that I could bring Father's business into a dreadful tangle today, just by indulging a fancy for finery."

"Is his business precarious, Abbie, or is finery prodigious?"

Abbie picked up a square of delicate lace. "That costs seventy-five dollars, Ralph."

"So? Do you want it?" Ralph reached into his pocket.

Abbie turned away from the counter. "Oh, no, Ralph!" she exclaimed. "I hope I never spend money that way." Then she added more lightly, "You are worse than Queen Ester here, and her advice is bewildering enough."

"But, Abbie, how can you be so absurd?" asked that young lady. "Those are not very expensive, I'm sure — at least not for you — and you certainly want some very nice ones. If I had one-third of your spending money, I wouldn't hesitate."

Abbie's low, sweet voice reached only her cousin's ear. "Ester, 'the silver and the gold are His,' and I have asked Him this very morning to help me be careful of what He has entrusted to me. Now do you think — ?"

But Ester had turned away and marched to the other end of the store, leaving Abbie to complete her purchases. She leaned against the door, tapping her fingers against the glass. How odd that in the smallest matters she and Abbie could not agree! How could the same set of rules govern them both?

The old question revived to be thought over anew. Clearly they were unlike — totally unlike. Now was Abbie right and she wrong? Or was Abbie — no, not wrong, the word certainly could not apply. There absolutely could be no wrong con-

nected with Abbie's way. Well, then, strange! She
was unlike other people, unnecessarily precise.
She studied the right and wrong of matters, which
Ester had never imagined had any moral implica-
tions at all.

While she waited and debated, her eye caught a
neat little cardholder hanging nearby, filled with
cards. Above it in gilt letters beckoned the words:

FREE TO ALL. TAKE ONE.

Ester's curiosity was piqued at the kind invitation. She drew a small, neat card from the case and
read:

I SOLEMNLY AGREE,
As God Shall Help Me:

1. To observe regular seasons of secret
prayer, at least in the morning and evening of each day.

2. To read daily at least a small portion of the Bible.

3. To attend one or more prayer meetings every week, if I have strength to get
there.

4. To stand up for Jesus always and
everywhere.

5. To try to lead at least one soul to
Jesus each year.

6. To engage in no amusement where
my Savior could not be a guest.

If the small bit of cardboard had been a coal of
fire, it could not have been dropped more suddenly on the marble floor than this was when Es-

ter's startled eyes understood its meaning. Who
could have written those sentences and then
placed them in a conspicuous corner of a fashionable store? Was she never to be at peace again?
Had the world gone wild? Did this emanate from
Cousin Abbie's brain, or were there more Cousin
Abbies in what she had supposed was a wicked
city? Or — O painful question, which haunted her
hourly now and all but chilled her blood — was
this religion, and did she have none of it? Was her
profession of Christianity a mockery, her life a lie?

"Is that thing hot?" Ralph asked in amusement
at her elbow.

"What? Where?" Ester looked about her.

"Why, that bit of paper — or is it a ghostly communication from the world of spirits? You look
startled enough for me to imagine anything, and it
spun away from your grasp so suddenly. Oh," he
added, as he quickly picked up the card and
glanced over it. "It is rather ghostly, I must confess,
or it would be if one were inclined that way. But I
imagined your nerves were stronger. Did the pronoun 'me' startle you?"

"How?"

"Why, I thought perhaps you considered yourself committed to all this solemnity before your
time. I must have one. Are you going to keep
yours?" He reached forward and pulled out one of
the cards. "Rather odd things to be found in our
possession, aren't they? Abbie now would be just
one of this type."

That cold shiver trembled again through Ester's
frame as she listened. Clearly he did not consider
her to be one of "that type." He had known her
only one day, and yet he seemed positive that she
stood on an equal footing with him. Oh, why was

it? How did he know? Was her manner then completely unlike that of a Christian, so much so that this young man saw it already? Or was some other action of hers inconsistent with his opinion of Christians? At this moment she would have given much to be back where she thought herself on certain questions two weeks ago. But she stood silent and let him talk, not once attempting to define her position — partly because this fearful doubt had crept into her mind, unaccompanied by the prayer:

> If I've never loved before
> Help me to begin today —

and partly, poor Ester, because she was so unused to confessing her Savior. She was not exactly ashamed of Him — at least she would have denied the charge indignantly. Yet it was much less confusing to remain silent and let others think as they would. This had been her rule, and she followed it now.

"Strange world this, isn't it?" Ralph continued. "How do you imagine our army would have prospered if one-fourth of the soldiers had been detailed for the purpose of coaxing the rest to follow their leader and obey orders? That's what it seems to me the so-called Christian world is up to. Does the comical side of it ever strike you, Ester? I can hardly keep from laughing now and then to hear the way in which Dr. Downing pitches into his church members, and they sit and take it as meekly as lambs brought to the slaughter. It does them about as much good, apparently, as it does me — no, not so much, for it amuses me and serves to make me good-natured and on congenial terms with myself for half an hour or so. I'm so glad, you see, that I don't belong to that set of miserable sinners."

"Dr. Downing does preach harsh sermons," Ester said at last, feeling the need to say something. "I have often wondered at it. I think they are contrived to do more harm than good."

"Oh, I don't wonder at it in the least. I'd make it sharper yet if I were he; the need exists evidently. If a fellow really means to do a thing, why does he wait to be punched up about it everlastingly? Hang me, if I don't like to see people act as though they meant it, even if the question is a religious one. Ester, how many times should I beg your pardon for using slang phrases? I fancied myself talking to my chum, delivering a lecture on theology, which is somewhat out of my sphere, as you have doubtless observed. Yet such people as you and I can't help having eyes and ears and using them now and then, can we?"

Still Ester kept silent, so far as defining her position was concerned. She was not ashamed of her Savior now, but of herself. If this lighthearted cousin's eyes were critical, she knew she could not bear the test. Yet she rallied sufficiently to condemn within her own mind the poor little cards.

They will do more harm than good, she told herself positively. To such young men as Ralph, for instance, what could he possibly want with one of them, except to make it a subject of ridicule when he got with some of his wild companions. But, as it turned out, his designs were not so wicked after all. As they left the store he took the little card from his pocket and handed it to Abbie with a quiet "Sis, here is something you will like."

Abbie read it. "How serious that is. Did you get it for me, Ralph? Thank you."

Ralph bowed and smiled on her a benign, almost tender smile, unlike the roguish twinkle that had shone in his eyes while he talked with Ester.

All through the busy day that silent, solemn card haunted Ester. It obstinately refused to be lost. She dropped it twice in their passage from store to store, but Ralph returned it promptly to her. At home she laid it on her dressing table. But pile scarves and handkerchiefs and gloves over it as high as she might, it was sure to flutter to the floor at her feet, whenever she hunted in the pile for some missing article. Once she seized and flung it from the window in her frustration and was rewarded by having Nancy present it to her about two minutes later, as a "something that landed square on my head, ma'am, as I was coming around the corner." At last she grew nervous over it and felt almost afraid to touch it, so entirely had it fastened itself on her conscience. Those great black letters in that first sentence seemed burned into her brain: "I solemnly agree, as God shall help me."

At last she deposited the unwelcome little monitor at the very bottom of her collar box under some unused collars. She told herself that it was for safekeeping so that she might not lose it again. She did not let her conscience say for a moment that it was because she wanted to bury the haunting words out of her sight.

CHAPTER XV

WHAT IS THE DIFFERENCE?

ster stood before her mirror, tucking in some stray braids of hair. She had retreated upstairs from the dining room just after dessert for that purpose. The family, along with Mr. Foster, was gathered in the back parlor. She was hurrying to join them.

"How things do conspire to hinder me!" she exclaimed as one loose hairpin after another slid softly and silently out of place. "This horrid ribbon doesn't match the trim on my dress either. Whatever has become of that blue one?"

With a jerk Sadie's "finery box" was produced and the contents riffled through. Methodical, orderly Ester was anxious to get down to that fascinating family group. The blue ribbon, however, with the waywardness of all ribbons, remained a silent and indifferent spectator of her trials, snugged back in the corner of a half-open drawer. Ester had set her heart on finding it, and the green collar box came next under inspection. Shoved

back toward its corner when the quest proved
vain, it seized the opportunity to tumble onto the
floor, showering its contents right and left.

"What next?" Ester muttered, as she scooped up
the scattered ruffles, collars, cuffs and laces. And
with them came the little card, face up, its bold,
black letters scorching their message into her very
soul: "I solemnly agree, as God shall help me."

Ester dropped the cuffs and laces out of her
hand and stood up, her heart beating wildly. What
did this mean? Was it merely coincidence that her
eyes had encountered this sentence so persistently
all this day, no matter where she put the card?
What was wrong with her anyway? Why should
those words hold such a strange power over her?
Why had she tried to block them out of her sight?

She read each sentence aloud slowly and carefully. "Now," she said, irritated that she was allow-
ing herself to be so bothered, "it's time to put an
end to this nonsense. I'm sick and tired of feeling
as I have lately. These are all very reasonable promises — at least, most of them are. I believe I'll adopt
this card. Yes, I will — that's what has been the
trouble with me. I've neglected my duty; that is, I
have so much responsibility and work at home that
I haven't had time to attend to it properly, but here
it's different. It's time for me to make a fresh start.
Tonight, when I come up to my room, I'll begin.
No, I can't do that either, for Abbie will be with me.
Well, at my first opportunity — no — I'll stop now,
this minute, and read a chapter in my Bible and
pray. There is nothing like the present moment for
keeping a good resolution. I like decision in everything — and, I daresay, Abbie will be very willing
to have a quiet talk with Mr. Foster before I come
down."

Sincerely desiring to be at peace with her newly troubled conscience — and sincerely sure that she was heading in the right direction for securing that peace — Ester closed and locked her door. She sat down by the open window in quite a self-satisfied state of mind to read the Bible and to pray.

Poor human heart, so entirely unaware of its own deep sickness — so willing to cover over the unhealed wound! Where should she read? She had always been a random reader of the Bible. But now with this fresh start it was important that she should take a more definite aim in her reading. She turned the leaves rapidly, eager to find a book that appeared inviting, and finally settled upon the Gospel of John as appropriate.

> In the beginning was the Word, and the Word was with God, and the Word was God.

Now that wretched hairpin is falling out again, as sure as I live, she moaned to herself. I don't know what is the matter with my hair today. I never had so much trouble with it.

> All things were made by Him; and without Him was not anything made that was made. In Him was life: and the life was the light of men.

There are Mr. and Mrs. Hastings. I wonder if they're going to call here? I wish they would. I'd like to get a closer look at that trim around her purse; it's lovely, whatever it is —

> And the light shineth in darkness; and

the darkness comprehended it not.

Now it was doubtful if it had once occurred to
Ester who this glorious "Word" was or that He had
anything to do with her. Certainly the wonderful
truths in these precious verses had to do with
every hour of her life. This evening they had not so
much as entered her busy brain. Yet she thought
she was doing the right thing to get rid of the
thoughts that had haunted her the past few days.
She was reading the verses aloud, and the
thoughts about the unruly hair and the trim on
Mrs. Hastings's purse remained thoughts, not to
become words — had they, perhaps even Ester
would have noticed the glaring incongruity. As it
was, she continued reading the verses and thinking the thoughts, until at last she paused.

Silence reigned in the room for several minutes.
Then a glow flushed over Ester's face. There she
sat, Bible in hand, one corner of the solemnly
worded card marking the verse at which she had
paused: "He came unto His own, and His own received Him not." And she realized that in the silence she had been thinking: Suppose Mrs.
Hastings should call and should inquire for her,
and she should go with Aunt Helen to return the
call. Should she wear Mother's black lace shawl
with her blue silk dress or simply the little ruffled
cape that matched the dress?

She read that last verse over again, with an uneasy feeling that she was not progressing very
well. Try as she would, Ester's thoughts seemed
resolved not to stay with that first chapter of John.
They roved all over New York, visited all the
places that she had seen and a great many that she
wanted to see. And, of course, there was the trim

on Mrs. Hastings's purse meandering through it all.

Suddenly Ester was startled by a tap at the door and Nancy's voice outside. "Miss Ried, Miss Abbie sent me to tell you there is company waiting to see you, and if you would please come down as soon as you can?"

Ester sprang up. "Very well," she replied. "I'll be down immediately."

Then she shut the card inside her Bible to keep the place and took a parting peep in the mirror to see that the brown hair and blue ribbon were in order. She wondered if it was really Mr. and Mrs. Hastings who called on her. Unlocking the door, she raced downstairs — vaguely aware that her intentions of setting herself right had not been carried out and that she had failed. Truly, after a lapse of so many years, the light was still shining in darkness.

In the parlor, after the other company had left, Ester found herself alone with Mr. Foster at the further end of the long room. Abbie, half sitting, half kneeling on an ottoman near her father, was engaged in an earnest conversation with him; her mother joined in from time to time, and Ralph laughed here and there. At their distance, however, they were unable to determine the subject of debate.

At last Mr. Foster turned to his nearest neighbor. "And so, Miss Ester, you manufactured me into a minister at our first encounter?"

In view of their closeness to being cousins Mr. Foster had discarded the formality of surnames. Ester had not yet recovered from the sense of awe he had at first inspired in her, so this opening sentence served only to embarrass her. She simply bowed in response.

"It's a dreadful curiosity on my part," continued Mr. Foster, "but I have an overwhelming desire to know why — or, rather, to know in what respect I am ministerial. Won't you enlighten me, Miss Ester?"

"Why," said Ester, growing more bewildered, "I thought — I said — I — no, I mean, I heard you talking with that old woman on the train, and some things you said made me think you must be a minister."

"What things, Miss Ester?"

"Everything," replied Ester, desperately searching about for the right words. "You talked, you know, about — about religion nearly all the time."

A look of absolute pain rested for a moment on Mr. Foster's face. "Has your experience with Christian men been so unfortunate that you believe no one but a minister ever converses on that subject?"

"I never hear any," Ester affirmed.

"But your example as a Christian lady, I trust, is such that it puts to shame your experience among gentlemen?"

"Oh, but," said Ester, still puzzled, "I didn't mean to confine my statement to gentlemen. I never hear anything like it from ladies either."

"Not from that dear old friend of ours on the train?"

"Oh, yes, she was different, too. I thought she had a strange way of speaking, but then she was old and ignorant. I don't suppose she knew how to talk about anything else. She is my one exception."

Mr. Foster glanced in the direction of the golden brown head that was still in eager debate at the other end of the room. "How is it with your cousin?"

"Oh, she!" said Ester, brought suddenly and painfully back to her troubled thoughts. After a moment's hesitation, she resolved to probe this matter to its root if it had one. "Mr. Foster, don't you think she is very peculiar?"

At which question Mr. Foster laughed a rich, deep laugh. His green eyes twinkled. "Do you think I am a competent witness on that subject?"

"Yes." Ester was too serious to be amused now. "She is entirely different from any person I ever saw in my life. She doesn't seem to think about anything else — at least she thinks more about this matter than any other."

"And that is being peculiar?"

"Why, I think so — unnatural, I mean — unlike other people."

"Well, let's see. Do you call it being peculiarly good or peculiarly bad?"

"Why," said Ester, perplexed, "it isn't bad, of course. But she — no, she is very good, the best person I ever knew. But it is being like nobody else, and nobody can be like her. Don't you think so?"

"I certainly do," he answered with the utmost gravity, and then he laughed again. Noticing her frustration, his voice took on a more serious note. "I think I understand you, Miss Ester. If you mean, don't I think Abbie has attained a high level of spiritual maturity for one of her age, I most certainly do. But if you mean, don't I think it almost impossible for people in general to gain as firm a foothold on the rock as she has, I certainly do not. It is within the power — it is, in fact, the blessed privilege, and even more it is the sacred duty — of every follower of the cross to cling as tightly and climb as high as she has."

"I don't think so," Ester said, with a decided

shake of her head. "It is much easier for some people to be good Christians than it is for others."

"Granted — there is a difference of temperament certainly. But do you rank Abbie among
those for whom it was naturally easy?"

"I think so."

This time Mr. Foster shook his head emphatically. "If you had known her when I first did, you
would not think so. It was very hard for her to
yield. Her natural temperament, her former life,
her circle of friends, her home influences were all
against her, and yet Christ triumphed.

"Yes, but having once decided the matter, it is
smooth sailing for her now."

"Do you think so? Does Abbie have no trials to
meet, no battles with Satan to fight, so far as you
can discover?"

"Only trifles," said Ester, thinking of Abbie's
family. But she decided that her cousin had luxu-
ries enough to offset these anxieties.

"You'll find that it needs precisely the same help
to meet trifles that it does to conquer mountains of
difficulty. The difference is in degree, not in kind.
But I happen to know that some of Abbie's 'trifles'
have been heavy and hard to bear. However, the
matter rests just here, Miss Ester. We are too willing to be conquered, too willing to be martyrs, yet
not willing to reach after and obtain the increasing
joys of the Christian life."

Ester was thoroughly uncomfortable. All of this
condemned her. At last, resolved to escape from
her awakening conscience, she pushed boldly on.
"People have different views on this subject as well
as on all others. Now Abbie and I do not agree in
our opinions. There are things which she thinks
right that seem to me quite out of place and im-

proper."

"Yes," he said graciously. "Would you object to mentioning some of those things?"

"Well, for instance, it was strange to hear her and other ladies speaking in your teachers' prayer meeting. I never heard of such a thing, at least not among cultured people."

"And you thought it improper?"

"Almost — yes, quite — perhaps. At least, *I* would never do it."

"Were you at Mrs. Burton's on the evening in which our group met?"

Mr. Foster's question surprised Ester; it seemed far off the subject. She concluded that he was absentminded or else had no response and was tired of the subject, so she answered simply and briefly in the affirmative.

"I was doing something else that night. Did many come?" he inquired.

"Quite a full group, Abbie said. The rooms were almost crowded."

"Was it pleasant?"

"Oh, very. I hadn't wanted to go since they were strangers to me, but I changed my mind and enjoyed the evening very much."

"Did people give reports?"

"Very lengthy ones. Mrs. Burton was particularly interesting. She had forgotten her notes but gave her reports beautifully from memory."

"Ah, I'm sorry for that. It must have ruined the evening for you."

"I don't understand, Mr. Foster."

"Why, you remarked that you considered it improper for ladies to take part in such activities. Of course, you couldn't have enjoyed what is improper."

"Oh, that's very different. It wasn't a prayer meeting."

"I beg your pardon. I didn't understand. It's only at prayer meetings that ladies shouldn't speak. Why?"

"Mr. Foster," Ester said sharply, "you know that it is quite another thing. There are enough gentlemen present, or ought to be, to do the talking in a prayer meeting."

"There is generally a large number of gentlemen at the teachers' meeting. I'm sure there were some present who could give Mrs. Burton's report."

"Well, I consider a teachers' meeting quite different from a gathering in a church."

"Ah, then it's the church that is at fault. If that's the case, I should propose holding prayer meetings in private parlors. Would that relieve your difficulty?"

"No," said Ester crossly, "not if there were gentlemen present. It is their business to conduct a religious meeting."

"Then, after all, it is religion that is at the foundation of the trouble. Pray, Miss Ester, was Mrs. Burton's report irreligious?"

"Mr. Foster," said Ester, her blue eyes flashing, "don't you understand me?" She clasped and unclasped her hands anxiously.

"I think I do, Miss Ester. The question is, do you understand yourself? Let me state the case. You are decidedly not a women's rights lady. I am decidedly not a women's rights gentleman — that is, in the general interpretation of that term. You would think, for instance, that Abbie was out of her realm in the pulpit or pleading a case at the bar. So would I. In fact, there are many public places in which you and I, for what we consider good reasons, would not like to see her. But, on the other hand, we both delight in Mrs. Burton's reports, whether verbal or written, as she may choose. We and many other ladies and gentlemen listen respectfully. We both like to hear Miss Ames sing, and we both consider it perfectly proper for her to entertain us at our social gatherings. At our literary society we have both relished Miss Hanley's exquisite recitation from 'Kathrina.' I'm sure not a thought of impropriety occurred to either of us. And we both enjoyed the conversations on the evening's subject, after the actual meeting had adjourned.

"So the question develops this way: It seems that it is pleasant and proper for fifty or more of us to hear Mrs. Burton's report in Mrs. Burton's parlor — to hear ladies sing — to hear ladies recite in their own parlors, or in those of their friends — to converse intimately on any sensible topic. But the moment the very same people are gathered in our chapel, and Mrs. Burton says, 'Pray for my class,' and Miss Ames says, 'I love Jesus,' and Miss Hanley says, 'The Lord is the strength of my heart, and my portion forever,' it becomes improper. Will you pardon my obtuseness and explain to me how that is so?"

But Ester was not in a mood to explain, if indeed she had anything to say. Her reply was curt: "I have never been accustomed to it."

"No! I think you told me that you were unaccustomed to hearing poetic recitations from young ladies. Does that condemn them?"

Ester sat there, confused, ashamed, annoyed. Her companion searched her face then roused himself from the sofa. Standing, he said, "Miss Ester, forgive me if I have seemed severe in my questions and sarcastic in my replies. I am afraid I have. The subject awakens sarcasm in me. It is so persistently twisted and misunderstood. Some of the finest people seem inclined to make our prayer meetings into formidable church meetings in order to hear a succession of not very short sermons, rather than into a social gathering of Christians to sympathize with and pray for and help each other, as I believe the Master intended them to be. But may I say a word to you personally? Are you quite happy as a Christian? Do you find your love growing stronger and your hopes brighter from day to day?"

Ester struggled within herself, tore bits of down from the edge of her fan and tried to regain her composure and her voice. But the tender, gentle, inquisitive tone had probed her inner being. The blue eyes that at last were raised to meet his open ones were melting into tears. "No, Mr. Foster, I am not happy."

"May I ask you why? Is the Savior untrue to His promises, or is His professed servant untrue to Him?"

Ester's heart was burning inside, and her conscience was whispering loudly, "Untrue, untrue." She had said nothing, when Ralph came briskly over to them.

"Two against one isn't fair play," he said, with both mischief and irritation in his tone. "Foster, don't shirk. You've taught Abbie — now go and help her fight it out like a man. Come, take yourself over there and get her out of this scrape. I'll take care of Ester. She looks as though she had been to camp meeting."

Mr. Foster, looking quizzically at Ralph and with concern at Ester, crossed to the other end of the long parlor where the voices were getting louder and one of them quite agitated.

CHAPTER XVI

A VICTORY

his is really the most absurd of all your recent absurdities," Aunt Helen was saying to Abbie in a loud, disgusted tone of voice as Mr. Foster joined the group.

"May I join you, and will you tell me what this particular absurdity is?" he asked, seating himself near Abbie's mother.

"Oh, nothing remarkable," that lady replied. "I guess it is quite time we were getting used to this new order of things. Abbie is trying to enlighten her father on the curious question of temperance, especially where it is connected with wedding parties, in which she is unusually interested just at present."

Abbie made an appealing glance in Mr. Foster's direction and otherwise remained silent.

"I can claim equal interest in the topic," he answered sunnily, "and will petition you, Mrs. Ried, to explain the point at issue."

"Indeed, Mr. Foster, I'm not a temperance lec-

148

turer and do not consider myself competent to perform the awful task. I refer you to Abbie, who seems to be fully informed and eager to display her argumentative powers."

Still Abbie kept silent. Only a close observer could tell by her moist eyes how deeply she felt the sharp tones and unmotherly words.

Her mother spoke at last more calmly. "My daughter and I, Mr. Foster, differ somewhat regarding the duties and privileges of a host. I have the right to set before my guests whatever I consider proper. She objects to the use of wine, as, of course, you are aware. Indeed, I believe she has imbibed her peculiar views from you. I've told her that since I have always entertained my guests with that beverage, I shall continue to do so."

Mr. Foster did not seem to be in the mood to argue the question but responded with good humor. "Ah, but, Mrs. Ried, you want to gratify your daughter in her parting request. That's only natural, isn't it?"

"We have gratified so many of her requests already that the whole thing strikes me as being the most ridiculous event that New York has ever witnessed. Imagine a dozen rough boys banging and shouting through my house, eating cake enough to make them sick for a month, to say nothing of how much they will stamp into my carpets — and all because they happen to belong to Abbie's mission class!"

Ralph and Ester had joined the group in the meantime.

"That last argument isn't valid, Mother," Ralph interjected. "Haven't I promised to clean the rooms myself, immediately afterward?"

Mr. Foster suddenly telegraphed a message to

Abbie, which she answered by stating in a low voice, "I should recall my invitations to them if that is the case."

"You will do no such thing," her father rejoined. "The invitations are issued in your parents' names, and we shall have no such senseless goings on connected with them. When you are in your own house you will no doubt be at liberty to do as you please. Until then it would be well to remember that you belong to your father's family at present."

Ralph was watching his younger sister's face. At this point he flung down the book he had been idly thumbing through. "It strikes me, Father, that you are making a tremendous din about a little matter. I don't object to a glass of wine myself, under almost any circumstances, and I think this excruciating sensitivity on the subject is ridiculous. At the same time I'd be willing to smash every wine bottle in the cellar at this moment, if I thought that Sis's last hours in the paternal mansion would be made any more peaceful by it."

During Ralph's harangue the elder Mr. Ried had grown ashamed of his rebuke. "I am precisely of your opinion, my son. We are making 'much ado about nothing.' We certainly have often entertained company before, and Abbie has sipped her wine with the rest of us without sustaining any significant injury, as far as I can see. And here is Ester, as staunch a church member as any of you, I believe, but that doesn't seem to forbid her behaving in a rational manner and partaking of whatever her friends provide for her entertainment. Why can't the rest of you be equally sensible?"

In the swift second of time between that sentence and her reply Ester had to endure three hard things: a sting from her restless conscience, a pained look from Mr. Foster and one of feigned shock from Ralph. Then her words tumbled out: "Indeed, Uncle Ralph, I beg you not to judge anyone else by my actions. I'm very sorry and ashamed that I've been so weak and wicked. I believe just as Abbie does, only I am not like her and have been tempted to do wrong, for fear you would think me foolish."

No one but Ester knew how much these sentences cost her, but the radiant look from Abbie's eyes was reward enough.

Ralph laughed outright. "Four against two! I've gone over to the enemy's side myself, you see, because of the pressure. Father, I advise you to yield while you can do it gracefully and also to save me the trouble of smashing the guilty bottles."

"But," persisted Mr. Ried, "I haven't heard an argument this evening. What is so shocking about a quiet glass of wine enjoyed with a select gathering of one's friends?"

Just then John presented himself at the door with a respectful "If you please, sir, there is a person in the hall who insists on seeing Mr. Foster."

"Show him in then," was Mrs. Ried's prompt reply.

John hesitated: "He is a very common looking person, sir, and — "

"She said to show him in, I believe," interrupted the gentleman of the house. His tone plainly indicated that he was venting on John the irritation he did not wish to bestow further on either his children or his guests.

John vanished, and Mr. Ried added, "You can take your *friend* into the library, Mr. Foster, if it proves to be a private matter."

Mr. Foster only bowed his reply.

John returned, ushering in a short, stout man dressed in a rough working suit. He fidgeted with his hat and shuffled his feet noiselessly on the plushly carpeted floors of the elegant parlor.

Mr. Foster turned to him at once and greeted him cordially. "Ah, Mr. Jones, good evening. I have been in search of you today but somehow managed to miss you."

Abbie slipped to his side and placed a small white hand in Mr. Jones's large coarse one. "How is Sallie tonight, Mr. Jones?"

"Well, ma'am, it is about her that I'm come, and I beg your pardon, sir" — turning to Mr. Foster — "for being so bold as to come up here after you. She is just that bad tonight that I could not find it in me to deny her anything. She is real anxious to see you. She has sighed and cried about it most of this day, and tonight we felt, her mother and me, that we couldn't stand it any longer. I said I'd not come home till I found you and told you how much she wanted to see you. It's asking a good deal, sir, but she is going fast, she is, and — "

Mr. Jones's voice broke, and he rubbed his rough hand across his eyes.

"I will be down immediately," Mr. Foster replied. "Certainly you should have come for me. I would have been very sorry indeed to disappoint Sallie. Tell her I will be there in half an hour, Mr. Jones."

And with a few added words of kindness from Abbie, Mr. Jones departed, sighing thankfully as he went.

"That man," said Mr. Foster, turning to Ester, as the door closed after him, "is the son of our old woman on the train. You remember I arranged for her to be carried safely to his home. My concern for her welfare was greatly relieved when I discovered that the son had become a faithful member of our mission Sunday school and was a thoroughly good man."

"And who is Sallie?" Ester inquired.

"Sallie is his treasure, a dear little girl, one of our mission scholars and a beautiful example of how faithful Christ can be to His little lambs."

"What is wrong with her?" Ralph asked.

This time Mr. Foster's face took on an unaccustomed sternness. "Sallie is a victim of our dreadful system of public poisoning. The son of her mother's employer, in a drunken rage, threw her from the top of a long flight of stairs, and now she lies warped and misshapen, mourning her life away.

"By the way," he continued, turning to Mr. Ried, "you asked for arguments to sustain my 'peculiar views.' Here is one of them: This man I've mentioned, whose crazed brain must answer for this young sad life and death, I happen to know for a fact began his downward career in a certain pleasant parlor in this city. He was among a select gathering of friends, taking a quiet glass of wine!"

Mr. Foster bid a hasty good night and left.

Ralph laughed nervously, when the family was alone: "Foster is very fortunate that an incident came to our very door to prove his theories."

Abbie had deserted her ottoman and taken a seat by her father's side. Now she laid her golden brown head lovingly against his shoulder and gazed into his stern gray eyes. "Father," she said softly, "you'll let your little curly have her own way just this time, won't you? I will promise not to coax you again until I want something very badly indeed."

Mr. Ried had decided on his plan of action some moments before. He was prepared to remind his daughter that he was *not* in the habit of playing the part of a despot in his own family. Since she and her future husband were so unyielding in their singular opinions, and so unconcerned about his wishes or feelings, he would, of course, not want to force his hospitalities on her guests.

He would have delivered his lecture but for one mistake. For just a moment he let his eyes meet the trusting blue ones. Whether he remembered that his one daughter was leaving her home soon or he thought of all the patient love and care she had shown him in those early morning hours, the stern gray eyes softened, and the hard lines about his mouth relaxed.

He ruffled the brown curls and said playfully, "Did you ever ask anything of anybody in your life that you didn't get?" More seriously he added: "You shall have your way once more. Abbie, it would be a pity to diminish your power at this late day."

"Fiddlesticks!" exclaimed her mother.

Before she could continue, Abbie was behind her chair, both arms wound around her neck. She kissed her quickly and gently on her cheeks, her chin and her nose.

"Nonsense!" her mother said, then she laughed. "Your father would consent to have the ceremony performed in the attic if you fancied that the parlors are too nicely furnished to suit your puritanic views. And I don't know that I might not be just as foolish."

"That man controls her completely," Aunt Helen sighed to Ester moments later as they stood together in the back parlor. "He is a first-class fanatic and grows wilder and more eccentric every day, and he bends Abbie to his slightest wish. My only consolation is that he is a man of wealth and culture and in every other respect is entirely acceptable."

After saying good night to the family, Abbie and Ester climbed the stairs together, said their prayers and went to bed. Ester, however, was still contemplating her aunt's "only consolation."

A new light dawned upon Ester. This was the secret of Abbie's "strangeness." Mr. Foster was one of those rare, wonderful men one occasionally reads about but almost never meets; Abbie was constantly under his influence and thus led by him. Few could expect to attain to such a level. Certainly she, with her own social disadvantage and unhelpful environment, could not hope to achieve it.

She was rapidly sinking back into her former self-satisfied state. She needed to do certain things. For instance, she should pay closer attention to that first chapter of John at her next reading and she should perform various other duties carefully. But on the whole Ester felt that she had worked herself up unnecessarily and that she must not expect to be perfect. And so once more a flag of truce was raised between her conscience and her life.

CHAPTER XVII

STEPPING BETWEEN

wo nights later Abbie, Ester, Ralph and Edwin Foster were lingering together for a few minutes in the sitting room. Their cheerful conversation was tinged with sadness. It was the evening before the wedding. Before this time tomorrow Abbie would have left them, and in a little while the ocean would roll between them. Ester sighed as she thought of it all. These enchanted three weeks, a step into a world of luxury and sophistication which she would never see again, were almost ended. Only two days remained before she would carry that same restless, unhappy heart back to the clattering dishes in that pantry and dining room at home.

Ralph broke the brief silence that had fallen between them. "Foster, listen to the sweet tones of that distant clock. It's the last time that you, as a free man, will hear it strike seven."

"Unless I prove to be an early riser tomorrow, which I may have to if I stay here longer. Abbie, I must be busy this entire evening. That funeral caused me to postpone some important business matters that I meant to have finished early in the day."

"It isn't possible that you have been to a funeral today! How you do mix things!" Ralph uttered in real or pretended horror.

"Why not?" Mr. Foster replied gently. "It is true though: life and death are strangely mixed. We laid our little Sunday school girl, Sallie, to rest today. It didn't jar as some funerals would have done; one had only to remember that she had reached Home. Miss Ester, if you will get that package for me, I will carry out your request with pleasure."

Ester hastened away to find the package, and Ralph, promising to meet him at the store in an hour, sauntered away. For a few moments Abbie and Mr. Foster talked together alone.

"Good-bye, both of you," he smiled, glancing over his shoulder at the two girls a short time later, his hat in hand. "Take care of her, Ester, until I relieve you. It won't be long now."

"Take care," Ester said cheerily. "You have forgotten the 'slip' that there may be 'between the cup and the lip.' "

He spoke to her with grave solemnity. "I never forget that wonderful expression that follows along the same lines: 'We know not what a day may bring forth.' But I always remember with great joy that God knows and will lead us."

"He is more serious than ten ministers," Ester said as they turned from the window. "Come, Abbie, let's go upstairs."

"I'll be up directly, Ester. I need to talk over a few last-minute details with Mother before tomorrow."

Two hours later Abbie entered the upstairs parlor where Ester awaited her. She curled herself into a small heap of white muslin at Ester's feet.

"There!" she laughed. "Mother has sent me away. She is thoroughly disgusted now. Dr. Downing is in the sitting room downstairs, and I have been guilty of going in to see him. Imagine such a fearful breach of etiquette in the Ried house! I don't know what to do with myself. There is really nothing more to do unless I eat the wedding cake."

"You don't act in the least like a young lady who is to be married tomorrow." Ester regarded her cousin with a half-amused, half-puzzled air.

"Don't I?" Abbie said, clapping her hand over her mouth and trying to look shocked. "What have I done now? I'm forever stepping out of line when it comes to manners. It will be a real relief to me when I am safely married and can lapse into being a common mortal again. Why, Ester, what am I guilty of now?"

"You are not a bit sentimental, are you, Abbie?"

Abbie laughed again. "Now don't, please, add that item to the list," she said merrily. "Ester, is it important to be sentimental on such an occasion? I wish you were married, I really do, so that you would tell me just how to behave. How can you and Mother expect me to be perfect when it is all so new to me?"

The merry look faded, and in its place tenderness filled the bright blue eyes. Her voice was low and quiet. "You think my mood is strange, I imagine, dear Ester — almost inappropriate. Perhaps it is, and yet I feel it's all right to be happy. The change is a serious one, but I've considered it for a long time.

"My new home will be close to my old one. My

brother will have a patient, faithful, lifelong friend in Mr. Foster, and this gives me more hope for him. I feel like quoting that verse, 'The lines have fallen unto me in pleasant places.' I can't pretend a sadness that I don't feel. Tonight the strongest feeling in my heart is gratitude. My heavenly Father has filled my cup to overflowing, so that it seems as if there is no room in my heart for — ," Abbie stopped abruptly.

"Ester, what on earth can be going on downstairs? Have you noticed the doors banging and people running up and down the stairs? If I weren't afraid of shocking Mother into a fainting spell, I would do some exploring."

"Suppose I go," Ester laughed. "Since it's not deemed proper for you to be about on the eve of your wedding, there can be no harm in my seeing what's going on downstairs. I'll let you know if it's anything very exciting."

In high spirits Ester closed the door on the young bride-elect and hurried below.

Chaos ruled the household. The air in the hall seemed charged with electricity. Loud but muffled voices were escaping from the front parlor. Ester knocked on the door. She heard her aunt cry, "Don't let her in!" Ester threw open the door.

"Oh, for mercy's sake, don't let her in," Aunt Helen cried again, rushing forward.

"Mother, hush!" Ralph cautioned. "It's only Ester. Where's Abbie?"

"In her room. What's the matter? Why are you all acting so strangely? I came to see why there's so much noise."

Her attention was immediately drawn to a group around the sofa: Uncle Ralph, Dr. Downing and, stooping over something she couldn't see, a

man who had been pointed out to her on an earlier
occasion as the great physician Dr. Archer.

"It is as I feared, Mr. Ried," said Dr. Archer. "The
pulse has ceased."

"It is not possible!" His hollow words echoed
through the room.

Then Ester saw the figure, pale and quiet, as it
settled into the calm of death. Mr. Foster! She stood
riveted to the spot in speechless horror. And then
the thoughts took shape into two woeful words:
"Oh, Abbie!"

What a household this was into which death had
so swiftly and silently entered! The quiet form of
Mr. Foster lay sleeping in the very room which was
decked out in festive beauty in honor of the bridal
morning — but there would be no bridal ceremony.

Ester shrank back in terror from the request that
she should go to Abbie. "I can't — I can't!" she said
over and over. "It will kill her. And, oh! It will kill
me to tell her."

Mrs. Ried was in a more hopeless state than Ester.

Mr. Ried cried out in agony, "What shall we do?
Is there no one to help us?"

Then Ester's cousin Ralph addressed Dr. Downing, who had withdrawn a little from the family
group. "It seems to me that you are our only hope
in this time of trial. You and my sister rely on, I
believe, the same power. The rest of us seem to
have no such help. Will you go to my sister, sir?"

Dr. Downing turned his eyes away from the still,
peaceful face which seemed to have fascinated him
and said simply: "I will do what I can for Abbie. It
is blessed to think what a Helper she has — One
who never fails. May God have mercy on those

who have no such friend."

They showed him to the brightly lit library and sent word to Abbie.

"Dr. Downing?" she said, turning briskly from the window in answer to Nancy's summons. "What do you suppose he wants of me, Nancy? I'm half afraid of him tonight. But I'll try to brave the ordeal. Tell Miss Ester to come up to me as soon as she can and be ready to defend me if I am to receive a lecture from him."

She said this as she passed to the door. Nancy was still standing near the window. A compassionate cloud hid the face of the August moon just then and veiled Nancy's own white, frightened face.

With what silent agony the family below waited and dreaded Dr. Downing's return or some message from that fateful room. The moments seemed to stretch into hours, and yet no sound did they make.

"She has not fainted then," muttered Ralph at last, "or he would have rung. Ester, you know what Nancy said. Couldn't you go to her?"

Ester cowered. "Oh, Ralph, don't ask me. I cannot."

Then silence prevailed. At last Dr. Downing opened the door. His moist eyes still shone, but his face reflected a wonderful peace.

"She knows all," he told Mr. Ried. "And the widow's God is hers. Mrs. Ried, she asks especially that she not see any living soul tonight, and, indeed, I think it will be best. And now, my friends, may I pray with you in this hour of trial?"

Skillful fingers prepared the sleeper in that front parlor for his long, long rest. And a group that had never before bowed the knee together knelt in the room just across the hall. Amid tears and moans they were commended to the care of Him who waits to help us all.

By and by a solemn quiet settled down upon the stricken household. In the front parlor the folding doors were closed, and the angel of death kept guard over his quiet victim. From the chamber overhead no sound came forth, and none knew save God how the struggle between despair and submission fared in that young heart. In the sitting room Ester waited breathlessly while Ralph gave the details, which she had not heard until now.

"We were crossing just above the store and had nearly gotten across. He was saying that he was completely ready for a long absence. 'It is a long journey,' he added, 'and if I never come back I have the satisfaction of thinking that I have left everything ready even for that. It is well to be ready even for death, Ralph,' he said, with one of his radiant smiles. 'It makes life more pleasant.' I don't know how I can tell you the rest."

Ralph's lips grew white and his face ashen. "Indeed, I hardly know how it was. An old, bent-over woman was crossing just behind us. Then a carriage came, and a wretch of a drunken driver pushed his way through. I don't know how Foster came to look around, but he did. Then he said, 'There is my dear old lady behind us, Ralph. She shouldn't be out with just a child for a companion.'

"Then he shouted in horror and sprang forward — I know nothing clearly that followed. I saw him drag that old woman fairly out from under the horses' feet. I heard the driver curse and saw him strike his frightened horses. They reared and plunged, and I saw him fall. But it all seemed to happen in a split second. How I got him home and got Dr. Archer and kept it from Abbie, I don't know. Oh, God, help my poor little darling." Ralph choked and stopped and wiped the great burning tears from his eyes.

"Oh, Ralph!" said Ester, as soon as she could speak. "Then all this misery comes because that driver was intoxicated."

"Yes," said Ralph, his white lips pressed together and his dark eyes flashing.

And that, knowing the time,
that now it is high time
to awake out of sleep:
for now is our salvation nearer
than when we believed.

Romans 13:11

CHAPTER XVIII

LIGHT OUT OF DARKNESS

Slowly, slowly, the night waned, and the eastern sky grew rosy with the blush of a new morning — the bridal morning!

How unreal, how impossible, it seemed to Ester. She pulled back the curtains and gazed drearily out upon the dawn. This was actually the day on which her thoughts had centered during the last three weeks. What a sudden halt had come to all their plans and preparations! How strange the house looked — one room decked out in festive beauty for the wedding and another with shrouded mirrors and billowy folds of crepe! Life and death, a wedding and a funeral — neither had touched so close to her before. Now one had suddenly glided backward and left her heart heavy with the coming of the other.

She turned mechanically to look at the silvery garment shimmering among the white furnishings of the bed. She was that very morning to have helped array the bride in those robes of beauty. Her own careful fingers had laid out all the accessories in the dressing room — sash and gloves and hand-kerchief and laces. She had stood in that very spot only yesterday and talked with Abbie. She had al-tered a knot of ribbons and given the ends a more graceful droop, and at that moment Abbie had been summoned to come downstairs to see Mr. Foster. Now he was waiting down there, not for Abbie, but for the coffin and the grave.

And Abbie was — here Ester gave a low moan and covered her eyes with her hands. Why had she entered that room at all? Why was all this pain allowed to come to Abbie? Poor, poor Abbie — she had been so happy and good, and Mr. Foster had been so entirely her guide — how could she ever endure it?

Ester doubted if Abbie could ever bear to see her again, because she had been so closely connected with all these splendid days over which such a pall had been cast. It would be very natural if she re-fused to see her — indeed, Ester almost hoped she would. This grief was too deep to be mentioned or endured, but with a quiet desperation she said, "Things must be endured." A wild thought filled her mind that if she could but have ordered the events, all this bitter sorrow would never be.

A low, timid knock interrupted her thoughts, and Nancy's swollen eyes and tearstained face ap-peared at the door with a message. "If you please, Miss Ester, she wants you."

"Who?" asked Ester with trembling lips and a sinking at her heart.

"Miss Abbie, ma'am. She asked for you and wishes that you will come to her as soon as you can."

Nothing had ever seemed so hard for her to do

— how to look, how to act, what to say and, above all, what not to say to this poor, widowed bride. These questions were by no means answered when she finally decided that if she must do it, the sooner it was over, the better. She rushed to get ready for the visit. Yet enough of Ester's personal self remained, even on that morning, to send a trickle of complacency through her veins, as she bathed her flushed face and smoothed her rumpled hair. Abbie had sent for her. Abbie wanted her. Evidently she had turned to her for help. As unable as Ester felt to give it, still it comforted her that she was the one selected from the household for companionship.

Ester knew that Aunt Helen had been with Abbie for a few minutes and that Ralph had slipped in and out again, too overcome to stay. But Ester had asked no question and received no information concerning her. She pictured her lying on the bed with disheveled hair and swollen eyes, either lost in her grief or in stony despair.

Just as she turned the doorknob and let herself into the morning room, which she and Abbie had enjoyed together, a clock in the hallway counted out twelve strokes. At twelve o'clock Abbie was to have become a wife!

Midway across the room Ester stopped. In the little easy chair by the open window, with one hand holding her place in the partially closed book, sat the young creature whose life had so suddenly darkened around her. The pure white morning robe was neat and simple; the golden brown curls were clustered softly around her brow. Abbie's deeply shadowed eyes were filled with tenderness.

Abbie held out her free hand to Ester, and a gen-

tle smile spread over her face. Ester stood transfixed as she might have done had she been one of
those who saw the angel sitting at the door of the
empty tomb. For only a moment she hesitated,
then she ran forward and dropped on her knees,
bowing her head over the white hand and the half-
open Bible and burst into tears.

"Dear Ester!" soothed Abbie.

"Oh, Abbie, Abbie, how can you bear it — how
can you live?" cried this friend who had come to
comfort the afflicted one!

Abbie was silent for a brief time. When she
spoke, there was a noticeable tremble in her voice.
" 'The Lord knoweth them that are his.' I'm trying
very hard to remember that. Christ knows it all,
and He loves me, and He is all-powerful. And yet
He is leading me through this dark road, so it must
be right."

Ester raised her eyes and dried her tears in
amazement. "But I don't understand — I don't see.
How can you be so calm and submissive, at least
right now — so soon — and you were to be married today?"

Abbie struggled with her feelings until only a
strange, almost death-like, pallor remained. She
clasped and unclasped her small hands, with a
mixture of pain and devotion in the movement.
Her white lips moved slightly, forming words that
met no mortal ear. Then she spoke again for Ester's
ears. "Dear Ester, I am praying. There's no other
way: I am praying all the time. I am keeping right
by my Savior. There is just a little, oh, a very little,
vale of flesh between Him and between my — my
beloved and me. Jesus loves me, Ester. I know it
now just as well as I did yesterday. I do not and
cannot doubt Him."

Ester did not — could not — move or speak.

Abbie remained quiet. Then her voice changed remarkably. "Ester, do you remember that we — he and I — stood together alone for a moment yesterday? I'll tell you what he said — the last words intended only for me that I shall hear for a little while. They are my words, you know, but I shall tell them to you so you may see how tender Christ is, even in His most solemn chastenings. 'See here,' he said, 'I will give you a word to keep until we meet in the morning: The Lord watch between thee and me while we are absent one from another.'

"I've been thinking, while I've been watching the dawning of this new day. This is his first day in heaven. Perhaps my long, long day will dawn on a beautiful morning like this. And I will say to him, as soon as I see his face again: 'The word was a good one. The Lord has watched between us, and the night is gone.' Think of it, Ester. I shall surely say that some day — 'some summer morning.'

The sweet faith this young Christian expressed in her jubilant words cannot be written down on paper. But, thank God, they can be in the heart — they are but the echo of those sure and everlasting words: "My grace is sufficient for thee." As for Ester, who had spent her years groveling in the dust of earth, she had not deemed this experience possible for humanity to reach. And still she knelt immovable and silent.

Abbie broke the silence yet again. "Dear Ester, I haven't seen him yet, and I want to. Mother doesn't understand, and she would not give her consent, but she thinks I'm safe while you are with me. Would you mind going down with me just to look at his face again?"

Oh, Ester would mind it dreadfully. She was

afraid of death. She was afraid of the effect such a scene might have upon this peculiar Abbie. She shivered with apprehension. How could her cousin ask that of her?

Before she could utter a word, Abbie's hand rested lovingly on her arm, and her low, sweet voice continued the pleading: "You don't understand my mood, Ester. I am not so unlike others. I wept bitterly last night. At times the pain was more than I could bear. I know that I will have more struggles, more pain. This is earth, and the flesh is weak. But right now my spirits are lifted up. And while I can still feel a faint glimmering of the glory that surrounds him, I want to look my last upon the dear clay which is to stay here on earth with me."

Ester arose and wrapped her arm about the tiny frame that held this brave, true heart. Without another word the two hastened down the stairs and entered the silent, solemn parlor. Ester's heart ached as she remembered how they had planned to descend the same staircase on this very day — in what a different manner and for what a different purpose. Apparently no such thought touched Abbie. She approached the still form without hesitation.

Ester hung back in the shadows of the parlor in almost breathless agony to see the result of this trial of faith and nerve. What a face it was upon which death had left its seal! No sculptured marble was ever so fine in its stolid beauty as was this clay-molded face; a smile of heavenly influence rested upon it.

Abbie, with her hands held tightly together and her lips parted slightly, drank in the smile. Then the sound of her voice echoed in low, musical tones in that great solemn room. "So he giveth his beloved sleep."

No other noise disturbed the silence. Abbie stood and gazed on the dear, dead face. And Ester waited near the door, anxiously watching the changing expressions on the scarcely less white face of the living. At last Abbie dropped upon her knees, wrapped in the soft white folds of her robe and clasped her hands over the lifeless breast. Then Ester's anxiety gave place to awe, and she noiselessly opened the door, stepped into the hall and left the living and the dead alone together.

Ester had to endure one more scene that day. Late in the afternoon, as she ventured into the closed room, an old woman was leaning over the motionless figure. How she had been permitted to enter, Ester did not stop to wonder. She had seen her only once before, but she recognized at once the worn, wrinkled face. A picture of the scene passed before her: the bent frame, leaning trustfully on the strong arm, which lay nerveless now; helped along through the pushing throng; reverently cared for as if she had been his mother. She had wondered then if she would ever see them again. Now she stood in the presence of them both; yet what an unmeasurable ocean had rolled between them!

The faded, tear-filled eyes looked up, and her shaking voice spoke her thoughts aloud to no one in particular: "He gave his life and was needed, oh, so much. But what am I saying? God let it be him instead of me, who wanted so to go. After trusting Him all along, am I at my time of life going to murmur at Him now? He came to see me only yesterday," she said more naturally now to Ester. "He told me good-bye. He said he was going on a long journey with his wife. And now may the dear Savior help the poor darling, for he has gone on his long journey without her."

Ester did not wait to hear more. The deep pain she had carried about with her all that weary day had reached its height with that last sentence: "He has gone on his long journey without her."

She fled from the room and upstairs to the quiet little chamber where she had been staying. She locked and bolted the door and began to pace up and down the room.

Not all of this pain that pounded so steadily in her heart was because of Abbie; at least not all of it was out of sympathy for her sorrow. A fearful tumult raged in her own soul; her last stronghold had been shattered. She had come to think that Abbie's Christian life was but a sweet reflection of Edwin Foster's strong, true soul and that she leaned not on Christ, but on the arm of flesh. She had told herself confidently that if she had such a friend as he had been to Abbie, she would be like her. In her anger and rebellion she had reminded herself that it was not strange for Abbie's life to be so free from blame; she had someone to turn to in her needs. Abbie could easily gloss over the petty trials of her life as long as she was surrounded and protected by that strong, true love. But now the arm of flesh had faltered, and the staff had broken — and only a moment before it was to become hers in name as well as in spirit.

Naturally, Ester had expected that the young creature, cut off from her best and dearest so suddenly, would faint and utterly fail. Instead she saw the triumph of the Christian's faith, rising even above death, sustained by no human arm and yet wonderfully sustained, even while she bowed for the last time over what was to have been her earthly all. The apathy that had numbed Ester all these years melted away, and for the first time in her life she saw with a thoroughly awakened soul that there was something in this Christian religion that Abbie had and she had not.

And thus it was that she paced her room in a twisted agony that was worse than grief and more poignant than despair. There was no use now in trying to lull her conscience back to sleep again. That time was past; it was entirely and acutely awake. The same all-wise hand that had tenderly freed one soul from its bonds of clay and called it Home had as tenderly and as wisely with the same stroke cut the cords that bound this other soul to earth. That hand had removed the scales from her long-closed eyes and broken the sleep that had nearly soothed her into ruin. And now her heart and brain and conscience were thoroughly and forever awake.

When at last from sheer exhaustion she stopped her excited pacing and sank into a chair, her heart was not more stilled. Long afterward, in remembering this hour, she felt she had been permitted to see more deeply into the recesses of her own depravity than any mortal had ever seen before. She began years back, at that time when she thought she had given her heart to Christ, and reviewed step by step all the weary way up to this present time. She found nothing but backslidings and inconsistencies and confusion — denials of her Savior, a closed Bible, a neglected closet, a forgotten cross. Oh, the bitterness, the unspeakable agony of that hour! Surely Abbie, on her knees struggling with her bleeding heart and yet feeling all around and underneath her the everlasting arms, knew nothing of desolation such as this.

Fiercer and fiercer waged the warfare, until at last every root of pride and complacency and every defense were utterly cast out. Yet Satan did not despair. Oh, he meant to have this poor sick, weak lamb, if he could get her; no stone should be left unturned, no arrow unshot. And when he found that she could be no more coaxed and lulled and petted into peace, he tried that darker, heavier temptation — tried to stupefy her into absolute despair.

No, she said in her heart, I am not a Christian: I have never been one; I can never be one. I've been a miserable, deceived hypocrite all my life. I wouldn't let myself be awakened. I have struggled against it. I have been only too glad to stop myself from thinking about it. I've been just a miserable stumbling-block with no excuse, and now I feel deserted, and rightly so. I don't deserve any rest. I have no Savior. I have insulted and denied Him. I have crucified Him again, and now He has left me to myself.

Thus did that father of lies pour into this weary soul the same old story he has repeated for so many hundreds of years with the same old foundation: "I — I — I." And, strange to say, this poor girl repeated the experience that has been lived many times in the past hundreds of years in the face of that other glorious pronoun, defying the old explanation: "Surely he hath borne our griefs and carried our sorrows. He was wounded for our transgressions; he was bruised for our iniquities. The chastisement of our peace was upon him: and with his stripes we are healed."

Yes, Ester knew those two verses. She knew yet another: "All we, like sheep, have gone astray. We have turned every one to his own way: and the Lord hath laid on him the iniquity of us all."

And yet she dared to sit with hopeless, folded hands and dark, despairing eyes and repeat that sentence: "I have no Savior now." Many a wandering sheep has dared, even in its repenting hour, to insult the great Shepherd in that way. Ester's Bible lay on the window seat — the large, somewhat worn Bible that Abbie had lent her to "mark just as much as she pleased." It lay open, as if it had opened by itself to a familiar spot. Heavy marks highlighted several of the verses, marks that Ester's pencil had not made.

Some power far removed from what had been guiding her desperate thoughts prompted her to reach for the book and focus on those marked verses. The words were these:

> For thus saith the high and lofty One that inhabiteth eternity, whose name is Holy; I dwell in the high and holy place, with him also that is of a contrite and humble spirit, to revive the spirit of the humble, and to revive the heart of the contrite ones. For I will not contend for ever, neither will I be always wroth: for the spirit should fail before me, and the souls which I have made. For the iniquity of his covetousness was I wroth, and smote him: I hid me, and was wroth, and he went on frowardly in the way of his heart. I have seen his ways, and will heal him: I will lead him also, and restore comforts unto him and to his mourners. I create the fruit of the lips; Peace, peace to him that is afar off, and to him that is

near, saith the Lord; and I will heal him.

Did an angel speak to Ester, or was it the dear voice of the Lord Himself? She didn't know. She only knew two phrases rang through her soul as the climax of all those wonderful words: "Peace, peace to him that is afar off," and "I will heal him."

In a moment, with the promise of the Crucified spread out before her, Ester was on her knees. She burst into passionate, tearful pleading, then settled into low, humble, contrite tones. Finally a peace stole into her prayer — the peace that comes only to those to whom Christ is repeating: "I have blotted out as a cloud thy transgressions, and as a thick cloud thy sins."

"Do you know, dear Ester," Abbie said, as they nestled close together that evening in the purple twilight, "heaven must have experienced two new joys today. They welcomed a newcomer to join those who walk with Him in white, because they are worthy. Then they shouted in triumph over another soul Satan has fought for and lost forever."

Ester smiled and whispered a soft "amen."

CHAPTER XIX

Sundries

eanwhile the days moved on. The time set for Ester's return home had long passed, and yet she stayed in New York.

Abbie clung to her, wanting her for various reasons. The unselfish mother far away, full of tender sympathy for the stricken bride, suppressed a sigh. She buried the thoughts of her own need for her eldest daughter's presence and help and wrote a long, loving letter to both the daughter and the niece; she gave her full consent to Ester's remaining away, so long as she could be a comfort to her cousin.

Two noteworthy items occurred during these days. The family had gathered for the first time at the dinner table, after the one who had been so nearly a son of the house had been carried to his rest in that wonderful treasured city. John was helping Ralph to his usual glass of wine. With a sharp, almost angry "No! Take it away and never offer me the accursed stuff again," Ralph refused it. "We would have had him with us today if it weren't for that. I'll never touch another drop of it as long as I live."

Mr. and Mrs. Ried heard the startling words but made no comment. They did, however, glance quickly at Abbie to see how she would bear this mention of her dead.

She looked into her brother's face, her eyes filling with tears. "Oh, Ralph, I knew it had a silver lining, but I did not think God would let me see it so soon."

Then the father and mother concluded that both their children were strange and that they did not understand them.

The other notable item produced a dissertation on etiquette from the mother.

Ralph and his father were in the back parlor. The son stood with one arm resting on the mantel while he talked with his father, who was ensconced in a great easy chair. Sitting in that easy chair in his own elegant parlor, with his handsome son standing before him in that relaxed position, was for the father synonymous with perfect satisfaction.

He frowned as the door opened noisily, and his wife entered in a huff. Ralph paused in the middle of his sentence and pushed a second easy chair forward for his mother. He returned to his former place by the mantel and waited patiently for the gathering storm to break into words. He didn't have long to wait.

"I really do not think, Mr. Ried, that this nonsense ought to be allowed. Besides being a very weird, unfeeling thing to do, it is positively indecent — and I think, Mr. Ried, that you ought to exercise your authority for once."

"If you would kindly inform me what you are talking about and where my authority is especially needed at this time, I might be persuaded to consider the matter," he said from the depths of the easy chair in his most provokingly indifferent tone.

His wife was too preoccupied to notice it and continued her deluge of words. "Here it is not even a week since he was buried, and Abbie has to make herself and her family seem perfectly ridiculous by appearing in public."

Mr. Ried came to an upright posture, and even Ralph was startled. "Where is she going?"

"Why, where do you suppose but to that absurd little prayer meeting, where she has always insisted upon going every Thursday evening. I used to think it was for the pleasure of a walk home with Mr. Foster. Why she should go tonight is beyond me!"

"Nonsense!" said Mr. Ried, settling back into the cushions. "A large public that will be. I thought at the very least she was going to the opera. If the child finds any comfort in such an atmosphere, where's the harm? Let her go."

"Where's the harm? Now, Mr. Ried, that shows how little you care for appearances sometimes. But at other times you can be quite as particular as I am. There is *nothing* Abbie might take a fancy to do that you would not side with her!"

"You're right about that, I suspect. At least I can't think of anything connected with her that couldn't be turned into just the right thing."

Mrs. Ried's retort was cut short by Abbie's entrance. She was dressed for a walk or a ride; the pallor of her face and the shadows under her dark eyes were enhanced by the deep mourning robes which fell around her like the night.

"Now, Abbie," said her mother, "I had hoped you would give up this outlandish whim. What will people think?"

"People are quite accustomed to seeing me there, dear Mother — at least all the people who will see me tonight. And if ever I needed help, I do just now."

"I should think it would be much more appropriate to stay at home and find help in the company of your own family. That's the way other people do when they are afflicted."

Abbie stared at her mother out of great solemn eyes. "Mother, I want God's help. No other will do me any good."

"Well," blustered her mother, "can't you find that help anywhere but in that plain, common little meetinghouse? I thought people with your peculiar views believed that God was everywhere."

The look of a hunted deer crossed Abbie's face and vanished as quickly as it had appeared. "Oh, Mother, Mother, you cannot understand," she moaned.

"At least I can understand this much," Mrs. Ried huffed. "My daughter is very anxious to do something that is absolutely unheard of, and I am thoroughly ashamed of you. If I were Ester I wouldn't like to support you in such a conspicuous parade. Remember, you have no one now but John to depend upon as an escort."

Ralph had remained a silent listener to the depressing conversation. In two short steps he was at his sister's side and encircled her trembling body with his strong arm. "In that last proposition you are quite mistaken, my dear mother. Abbie happens to have a brother, who considers it an honor to go with her anywhere she wants to go."

Mrs. Ried surveyed her tall, haughty son in genuine astonishment. For once she was silent.

"Oh," she said at last, "if you have chosen to rank yourself on this ridiculous fanatical side, I have nothing more to say."

As for the father, one hand was shading his eyes while he regarded the pallid face of his curly-haired darling and looked through half-closed fingers, either unaware of or indifferent to the talk that was going on.

But will Ralph ever forget the sweet smile that illumined the pure, young face of his sister as she turned to him?

Thereafter a new era dawned in Abbie's life. Ralph, for reasons best known to himself, chose to be released from his vacation engagements in a neighboring city and remained at home. Abbie went as usual to her mission class, to her Bible class, to the teacher's prayer meeting, to the regular church prayer meeting — everywhere she had been accustomed to going. And she was always and everywhere accompanied and encouraged by her brother.

As for Ester, these were days of great opportunity and spiritual growth to her. A new joy had taken root in her heart and shone forth upon her countenance.

We span the weeks between and reach the afternoon of a September day, bright and beautiful, as the month draws to a close. Ester is sitting alone in her room in a comfortable chair by the open window. In her lap lies an open letter. She seems to be reading her heart, not the letter, which has come from Sadie.

My dear city sister,

Mother said tonight, as we were promenading around the dining room for the sake of exercise — and also to clear off the table (Maggie had a toothache and was off-duty): "Sadie, my dear child, haven't you written to Ester yet? Do you think it is quite right to neglect her so, when she must be very anxious to hear from home?"

Now, you know, when Mother says, "Sadie, my dear child," and looks at me from those reproachful eyes of hers, there is nothing short of mixing a mess of bread that I would not do for her. So here I am: place, third story front; time, 11:30 p.m.; position, foot of the bed (Julia is sleeping at the head), one gaiter off and one gaiter on, somewhat after the manner of 'my son John' so renowned in history.

Speaking of bread, how abominably that article can act. I had a solemn conflict with a batch of it this morning. First, you must know, I forgot it. Mother assured me it was ready to be mixed before I awakened, so it must have been before that event took place that the forgetting occurred. Be that as it may, after I was thoroughly awake — and up — and down, I still forgot it. The fried potatoes were frying themselves fast to that dreadful black dish they are put in to sizzle. And that, by the way, is the most nefarious thing in the entire kitchen list to get clean (except for the dishcloth). Well, as I was saying, the potatoes burned themselves, and I ran to the rescue.

Then Minnie wanted me to go to the yard with her to see a "dear dunning little brown and gray thing, with some greenish spots, that walked and spoke to her." The interesting stranger proved to be a frog!

While examining and explaining in detail the nature, character and occupations of the entire frog family, the mixture in the tin pail behind the kitchen stove took that opportunity to sour. My! What a bubble it was in, and what a curious odor it emitted, when at last I returned from frogdom to the ordinary pursuits of life and gave it my attention. Maggie was above her elbows in the washtub, so I seized the pail and in dismay dashed up two flights of stairs in search of Mother. I suppose you know what followed. I assure you, I think mothers and soda are splendid! What remarkable institutions those ingredients are.

While I made sour into sweet with the aid of its soothing proclivities, I moralized. The result of that was that after I had squeezed and mushed and thumped and patted my dough the required number of times, I tucked it away under blankets in a corner.

Then I ventured out to the piazza to ask Dr. Douglass if he knew of an article in the entire round of *Materia Medica* which could be given to human beings when they were sour and disagreeable and which, like soda in dough, would immediately work a reform. He acknowledged his utter ignorance of any such principle. I then advanced the idea that cooking was a much more developed science than medicine; an animated discussion followed.

Meanwhile, what do you suppose that bread was doing? Just spreading itself in the most remarkable manner over the nice blanket under which I had cuddled it! Then I had an amazing time. Mother said the patting process must all be done over again, so there was abundant opportunity for more moralizing. That bread developed the most extraordinary stick-to-i-tiveness I ever beheld. I assure you, if total depravity is a mark of humanity, then I believe my dough is human.

Well, we are all still alive, though poor Mr. Holland is, I fear, very little more than that. He was thrown from his carriage one evening last week and brought home insensible. He is now in a raging fever and very ill indeed. For once in their lives both doctors agree. He is delirious most of the time, and his delirium leads him to imagine that only Mother can do anything for him. The doctors think he imagines she is his own mother and that he is a boy again. All this makes matters rather hard on Mother. She is frequently with him half the night. Often Maggie and I are left to reign supreme in the kitchen for the entire day. Those are the days that 'try men's souls,' especially women's.

I am sometimes tempted to think that all the book knowledge in the world is not to be compared to knowing just what and how and when to do in the kitchen. I especially think so for a few hours when Mother, after a night of keeping watch in a sickroom, comes down to undo some of my blundering. She is the most patient, dearest, most loving, kindest mother that ever a mortal had. Because she is so patient I will rejoice over the day when she can give a little sigh of relief and leave the kitchen, calm in the assurance that it will be right-side-up when she returns.

Ester, how did you make things go right? I'm sure I try harder than I ever knew you to, and yet salt will get into cakes and puddings and sugar into potatoes.

Just here I'm conscience smitten. I beg you not to construe one of the above sentences as having the remotest allusion to your being sadly missed at home. Mother said I was not even to hint at such a thing, and I'm sure I haven't. I'm a remarkable housekeeper. The fall term at the academy opened week before last. I have hidden my schoolbooks behind that old barrel in the northeast corner of the attic. I thought they would be safer there than downstairs. At least I was sure the bread would do better in the oven because of their ascent.

To return to the scene of our present

trials: Mr. Holland is, I suppose, very dangerously sick, and poor Mrs. Holland is the very embodiment of despair. When I look at her in prospective misery, I am reminded of our poor, dear cousin Abbie (to whom I would write if it didn't seem a sacrilege). I conclude there is really more misery in this world of ours than I had any idea of. I've discovered why the world was made round. It must be to typify our lives — sort of a treadmill existence, you know. We come constantly around to the things we thought we had done yesterday and put away, and we relive today the sorrows we thought were vanquished last week. I'm sleepy, and it is nearly time to bake cakes for breakfast. 'The tip of the morning to you,' as Patrick O'Brien greets Maggie.

Yours nonsensically,
Sadie

CHAPTER XX

At Home

ver this letter Ester had laughed and cried and finally become lost in quiet thought. Abbie came in after a little while and with a quizzical look settled on an ottoman in front of her. Ester placed the letter in her hands without comment. Abbie read it and laughed considerably, then she grew more sober and at last folded the letter.

"Well," Ester said, smiling a little.

"Oh, Ester."

"Yes, you see they need me."

A lively, yet sad talk followed, and then a moment of silence fell between them, until Abbie broke it with a sudden question: "Ester, isn't this Dr. Douglass gaining some influence over Sadie? Have I imagined it, or does she speak of him frequently in her letters, in a way that gives me an idea that his influence is not for good?"

"I'm afraid it is very true. His influence over her seems to be great, and it certainly is not for good. The man is an infidel, I think. At least he is very far

187

indeed from being a Christian. I read a verse in my Bible this morning which, when I think of my past influence over Sadie, reminds me bitterly of myself. It went like this: 'While men slept, his enemy came and sowed tares — .' If I had not been asleep I might have won Sadie for the Savior before this enemy came."

"Well," Abbie answered gently, not in the least contradicting her statement, "you will try to undo all that now."

"Oh, Abbie, I don't know. I am so weak — like a child just beginning to take little steps alone, instead of being the strong disciple I might have been. I distrust myself. I am afraid."

"I'm not afraid for you," Abbie affirmed. "In the first place you are not like a little child: you must never even try to take one step alone. And besides, there are more verses in the Bible than that one. See here, let me show you mine."

Abbie produced her little pocket Bible and pointed with her finger while Ester read: "When I am weak, then am I strong." Then turning the pages rapidly, as one familiar with the strongholds of that tower of safety, she pointed again. Ester read: "What time I am afraid, I will trust in thee." A sweet smile spread across Ester's fair face.

It was a sultry October day, one of those days which may appear during that golden month, like a last turning back of the calendar to the departing summer. When that kind of day comes to people who have hard, stressful work in the stifling heat of summer, they become thoroughly uncomfortable, not to mention cross.

At almost five o'clock in the dining room of the other Ried household, Sadie was rushing back and forth — much as Ester had on so many evenings — but there was not as much method in Sadie's rushing. The curtains were raised as high as the tapes would take them, and the slant rays of the yellow sun were pouring in, doing their bravest to melt the balls of butter on the table into oil. Poor, tired, bewildered Sadie had forgotten to let down the shades and forgotten the ice for the butter, laid out the tablecloth crookedly and found no time to straighten it. This had been one of her trying days. Mrs. Ried's care of Mr. Holland had been earnest and unremitting, and Sadie, in her unaccustomed role of mistress downstairs, had reached the verge of exhaustion.

She glanced nervously at the inexorable clock as she flew back and forth. Among Mrs. Ried's boarders were some whose business required them to be served promptly at five o'clock. Maggie had been summoned to carry out an urgent errand connected with the sickroom. And Sadie, our inexperienced butterfly with her wings drooping, was trying to gather her wits enough to ready the dreadful tea table for the thirteen boarders who were waiting to be summoned.

"What did I come after?" she asked impatiently, her hand on her frowning forehead as she glanced about the pantry trying to decide what had brought her there in such hot haste. "Oh, a spoon — no, a fork, I guess it was. Why, I didn't remember the forks at all. As sure as I'm here, I believe they are here, too, instead of being on the table. And, oh, my patience, I believe those biscuits are burning. I wonder if they are done. Oh, dear me!" The young lady, Mr. Hammond's star scholar, bent over the indignant oven with a bewildered and burning face to check the state of the biscuits and inhaled hot whiffs of steam.

It was such an engrossing task that she didn't hear the sound of carriage wheels near the door nor the banging of trunks on the side piazza. She was halfway across the dining room, with a tin of puffy biscuits in her hands and the doubtful look still on her face when she felt the touch of two soft, loving arms around her neck. Spinning around, she screamed, "Oh, Ester!" And at once setting the tin of biscuits on one chair and herself on another, Sadie covered her face with both hands and cried.

"Why, Sadie, you poor dear child, what can be the matter?" Ester had never seen tears on that happy young face. She laid a soothing hand on Sadie's arm.

But Sadie's first remark drove away Ester's concern. Springing to her feet, Sadie looked anxiously on the chair full of biscuits.

"Oh, Ester," she said, "are these biscuits done, or will they be sticky and horrible in the middle?"

How Ester laughed! "Done — of course they are, and beautifully, too. Did you make them? Here, I'll take them out. Sadie, where is Mother?"

"In Mr. Holland's room. She has been there nearly all day. Mr. Holland is no better, and Maggie has run an errand for them. Why have you come? Did the angels send you?"

"Where are the children?"

"They have gone on a walk. Little Minnie wanted Mother every other minute, so Alfred and Julia have carried her off with them. Say, you dear Ester, how did you happen to come? How shall I be glad enough to see you?"

Ester laughed. "Then I can't see any of them," she said in response. "Never mind, then we'll have some tea. You poor child, how very tired you look.

Just sit in that chair, and see if I have forgotten how to work."

Sadie, who was more worn out and over-wrought than she had ever thought possible, leaned back in her mother's chair with a delicious carefree air and watched a wonderful spirit take possession of the room. Down came the shades in a twinkling, and the low red sun peeked in on them no more. The tablecloth straightened itself. Pickles and cheese and cake got out of their confused proximity, and each one marched to its appropriate niche on the neatly set table. A flying visit into well-known regions brought forth hard, sparkling, ice-crowned butter. When at last the fragrant tea stood ready to be served, and Ester, bright and smiling, stationed herself behind her mother's chair, Sadie gave a little relieved sigh, and then she laughed.

"You're straight from dreamland, Ester — I know it now. That tablecloth has been crooked in spite of me for a week. Maggie lays it down, and I cannot straighten it. I never get to it. I travel five hundred miles every night to get this supper ready, and it's never ready. I have to pop up for a fork or a spoon, or I set out four plates of butter and none of bread. Oh, there is clever work about it, and none but thoroughbred miracle-workers can get every little insignificant, indispensable thing on a table. I can't keep house."

"You poor kitten," Ester said gently, feeling very sympathetic for this pretty young sister and very glad indeed that she had come home. "Who would think of expecting a butterfly to spin? You shall bring those dear books down from the attic tomorrow. In the meantime, where is the tea bell?"

"Oh, we don't ring," said Sadie. "The noise disturbs Mr. Holland. Here comes my first lieutenant, who takes charge of that matter. My sister, Miss Ried, Dr. Douglass."

Ester returned the deferential bow bestowed upon her. She felt the renewed anxiety she had experienced lately when she thought of this dangerous stranger in connection with her beautiful, giddy, unchristian sister.

On the whole, Ester's homecoming was pleasant. To be sure, it was a remarkable change from her recent life; the faintest bit of a sigh escaped her lips as she pulled off her dainty cuffs and prepared to wipe the dishes while Sadie washed, and Maggie finished her interrupted ironing. What would John, the trim and properly trained waiter at Uncle Ralph's, think if he could see her now? How funny Abbie would seem engaged in such a task!

Sadie looked so relieved and rested and chatted so happily that presently Ester sighed again. "Poor Abbie! How very, very lonely she must be tonight. I wish she were here for you to cheer her, Sadie."

Later, while she dipped into the flour before relieving Sadie of her fearful task of sponge setting, the kitchen clock struck seven. This time she laughed at the contrast. They were probably just going down to dinner now at Uncle Ralph's. Only night before last she was there herself. She had been out shopping that day with Aunt Helen. She was dressed in the lovely blue silk with the real laces, a gift from Aunt Helen, and the tiny pearl, Abbie's last gift, that fastened the silk at the throat.

They were sitting down to dinner without her, and she was in the great pantry five hundred miles away. A long, wide calico apron covered her traveling dress, her sleeves were rolled above her elbows, and she was scooping flour out of the barrel into a big wooden bowl!

My, how her mother's weary face had brightened with surprise as she caught the first glimpse of her. How lovingly she had enfolded her in those dear motherly arms and cried: "My dear daughter! What an unexpected blessing and what a kind Providence that you have come just now."

Then Alfred and Julia had been as eager and jubilant in their greeting as though Ester had always been the perfect sister to them. And little Minnie crumpled Ester's dainty collar into an unsightly rag and bestowed upon her "Scotch kisses," "Dutch kisses," "Yankee kisses" and genuine, sweet baby kisses in her uncontrollable glee over dear "Auntie Essie."

And, oh, this Ester Ried who had come home was not the Ester Ried who had departed from them only two months ago! A whole lifetime of experience and instruction seemed to have been crowded into those two months. But nothing of her past awakened more keen regret in this young girl's heart than the thought of her undutiful, unsisterly life. It was all to be different now. She thanked God that He had let her return to that very kitchen and dining room to undo her former work.

The old sluggish, selfish spirit had left her. Before this she had done everything for Ester Ried; now she was to do it for Christ — everything, even the mixing up of that flour and water. Wasn't the word given: "Whatsoever ye do, do all to the glory of God"? How broad was that word *whatsoever*. Why, that covered every movement, yes, and every word. How could life have seemed to be dull and uninteresting and profitless? How could she have missed its joy?

Sadie hushed her busy tongue that evening as

she saw Ester kneeling in the moonlight to pray. A kind of awe stole over her when she realized that the kneeler seemed unconscious of any earthly presence. Somehow it struck Sadie as distinct from any kneeling she had ever watched in the moonlight before.

Ester rested her tired, happy head on her own pillow and felt this word ringing sweetly in her heart: "And ye are Christ's and Christ is God's."

CHAPTER XXI

TESTED

ster was winding the last smooth coil of hair around her head when Sadie opened her eyes the next morning.

"My!" she said. "Do you know, Ester, it is perfectly delightful to lie here and see you and remember that I shall not be responsible for those cakes this morning! They shall want a pint of soda added to them for all that I shall need to know or care."

Ester laughed. "You will surely have your own pantry well stocked with soda someday. It seems to have made a very strong impression on your mind."

She had come home to help; her mother and Sadie would realize after this how much of a helper she could be. That very day should be the beginning of her old, new life. It was baking day — her most hated before, her pleasure now. She could choose no more useful day. How she would dispatch the pies and cakes and biscuits, to say nothing of the wonderful loaves of bread. She smiled cheerily on her young sister, as she recognized in part the burden she was about to lift from her shoulders.

By the time she was ready for the duties of the day she had relived in her imagination the entire routine of that busy, happy day. She left her little clothespress wrapped in armor — the pantry and kitchen were to be her battlefield where she would encounter a whole host of old temptations and trials to be vanquished.

Thus Ester planned, and thus it happened that she did not once enter the kitchen during all that long day. Sadie's young shoulders bore more of the hundred little burdens of life that Saturday than they had ever carried before.

Descending the stairs, Ester met Dr. Van Anden for the first time since her return. He greeted her with a hurried "good morning," as if he had just seen her the day before. He at once pressed her into service: "Miss Ester, will you go to Mr. Holland immediately? I cannot find your mother. Send Mrs. Holland from the room — she excites him. Tell her I said she is to come immediately to the sitting room; I wish to see her. Give Mr. Holland a half teaspoonful of the mixture in the drinking glass every ten minutes. On no account leave him until I return, which will be as soon as possible."

Certain that his directions would be followed, the doctor vanished.

For about a quarter of a minute Ester wavered. Dr. Van Anden's tone and manner were filled with his usual authority — a habit of his that had always annoyed her. She shrank almost with terror from entering a dark, quiet room and assuming the role of nurse. Her base of operations, by choice, had been the light, airy kitchen, where she felt needed at this very moment.

Ester had of late secured one Bible verse as part of her armor to go with her through each day. On this particular morning the verse was, "Whatsoever thy hand findeth to do, do it with thy might." Now if her hands found work waiting for her down this first flight of stairs instead of down two, as she had planned, what was that to her? Ester proceeded immediately to the sickroom, dispatched the almost frantic wife according to the doctor's peremptory orders, gave the mixture as directed and waited patiently for the doctor's return — whereupon she heard herself installed as head nurse for the day. She was given just enough time to eat a very hurried second meal at the table with Sadie. There she listened to her half-pitiful, half-comic complaints and learned that her mother was down with a sick headache.

So it was that this first day at home drew toward its close. Not one single thing that Ester had planned to do, and do well, had she been able to accomplish. It had been a test for her to sit there patiently and watch the slow breathing of that almost motionless man on the bed before her; to rouse him at set intervals to pour some mixture down his unwilling lips; to fan him occasionally, and that was all. It had been difficult, but Ester had not chafed under it. She had recognized the necessity — no nurse to be found, her mother sick, and the young, frightened, worn-out wife not to be depended upon for help. Clearly she was at her post.

So as the red sun whispered a good night from a little corner of the closed curtain, it found Ester not angry, but very sad. Such a weary day! This man on the bed was dying; both doctors had shown that in their expressions at least a dozen times that day.

How her life of late was being mixed up with death. She had just passed through one sharp lesson, and here at the threshold awaited another. This was different from that last though — oh, very different — and herein lay some of the sadness.

Mr. Foster had said that "everything was ready for the long journey, even if there should be no return." Then she recalled the look of glory on that marble face and heard again that wonderful sentence: "So he giveth his beloved sleep." But this man here! He had not made everything ready. So at least she feared. Professed Christian though she had been and living in the same house with him for so many years, she was aware that she knew very little about him. She had seen much of him and talked much with him, but she had never mentioned to him the name of Christ, the name after which she called herself.

The sun sank lower and was almost gone, the weary day nearly done. This young watcher felt that the day begun in brightness was now closing in gloom. It was not such a clear path as she had thought; some things she could not undo. Those days of opportunity, in which she might at least have invited this man to Jesus, had passed; it seemed altogether probable that another would never come.

She heard a little rustle of the drapery about the bed and whirled around to meet the great searching eyes of the sick man, fixed upon her. Then he spoke in hushed, but distinct tones. "Am I going to die?"

Oh, what was Ester to say? How his eyes searched her soul! She could not tell him no, and it seemed equally impossible to say yes. So the silence was unbroken, while every nerve in her body seemed to tremble. She felt her face blanch under the steady gaze of those mournful eyes. At length the silence answered him, for he turned his head from her and half buried it in the pillow. Neither spoke nor moved.

That awful silence! That moment of opportunity, perhaps the last on earth for him — perhaps it was given to her to utter the last words he would ever hear from mortal lips. What could she say? If she only knew how — if she only had the right words. Yet something must be said.

Then there came to Ester one of those marked Bible verses which had recently become so precious. Her hushed, clear voice filled the room.

"God is our refuge and strength, a very present help in trouble."

No sound from the quiet figure on the bed. She could not even tell if he had heard, yet perhaps he might have; so she gathered them in a little string of wondrous pearls and let them fall with a gentle cadence from her lips.

"Commit thy way unto the Lord; trust also in him, and he shall bring it to pass."

"The Lord is nigh unto all them that call upon him — the Lord is gracious, and full of compassion."

"Thus saith the Lord, your Redeemer, the Holy One of Israel, I, even I, am he that blotteth out thy transgressions for mine own sake, and will not remember thy sins."

"Look unto me and be ye saved, all ye ends of the earth; for I am God, and there is none else."

"Incline your ear, and come unto me; hear, and your soul shall live."

Ester was quiet for a moment, and then she re-

peated the little verse that embodied for her all
that was tender and soothing and wonderful:
"What time I am afraid I will trust in thee." Was
this man, who was edging to the very brink of the
river, afraid? Ester didn't know, nor was she to
know whether those gracious invitations from the
Redeemer of the world had fallen on unheeding
ears, or not. With a little sigh both of relief and of
sorrow that the opportunity was gone, she turned
to meet Dr. Van Anden. He sent her out into the
light and glory of the departing day, to catch a bit
of its freshness.

At the last midnight stroke of that long, long
day, they were gathered about the bed. Sadie was
there, solemn and awestruck. Mrs. Ried had arisen
from her couch of suffering and nerved herself to
be a support to the poor young wife. Dr. Douglass,
at the side of the sick man, kept watch over the
fluttering pulse. Ester, on the other side of the bed,
looked on in helpless pity, and other friends of the
Hollands were grouped about the room. So they
watched and waited for the swift arrival of the
death angel. The death dampness had gathered on
his brow, and the pulse seemed but a faint tremble
now and then. Those whose eyes were used to
death thought that his lips would never frame
mortal sound again.

Suddenly the eyelids raised, and Mr. Holland
stared at the blue eyes that peered at him from the
foot of the bed. Ester had slipped there to make
more room for her mother and Mrs. Holland. In a
clear, distinct tone, one unmistakable word came
forth: "Pray!"

Will Ester ever forget the terror that coursed
through her when she felt that look and heard that
word? She glanced quickly about her. She and her

mother were the only ones who probably ever prayed. Could she, would she, that gentle, timid, shrinking mother? But Mrs. Ried was attending to the now almost fainting Mrs. Holland.

"He says pray!" Sadie murmured. "Oh, where is Dr. Van Anden?"

Ester knew he had been called to an emergency at the house across the way. Before he could return, this waiting spirit might be gone — gone without a word of prayer. Would Ester want to die in such a manner, with no voice to cry out for her to that listening Savior? But then no human being had ever heard her pray. Could she? Must she? Oh, for Dr. Van Anden — a Christian doctor! Oh, if that infidel stood anywhere but there, with his steady hand clasping the fluttering pulse, with his cool, calm eyes gazing curiously on her

But Mr. Holland was dying. Perhaps the everlasting arms were not underneath him. At this fearful thought, Ester dropped upon her knees, giving utterance to her deepest need, "Oh, Holy Spirit, teach me just what to say!"

Her mother listened, startled by the familiar voice, and could only think that petition was answered.

Ester felt it in her soul. Dr. Douglass, her mother, Sadie — it seemed as if no one else was there, only this dying man and Christ and she, pleading that the passing soul might be met even now by the angel of the covenant.

There were those in the room who never forgot that prayer of Ester's. Dr. Van Anden, entering hastily, paused midway in the room, took in the scene and then was on his knees, uniting his silent petitions with hers. So fervent and persistent was the cry for help that even the sobs of the stricken

wife were hushed in awe. Only the watching doctor, with his finger on the pulse, knew when the
last fluttering beat died out, and the death angel
pressed his triumphant seal on the pallid lip and
brow.

"Dr. Van Anden," Ester said the next morning,
as they waited in the death chamber for Mrs.
Ried's directions, "was — did he," motioning toward the silent occupant of the couch, "did he ever
think he was a Christian?"

The doctor shook his head sadly.

"Oh, doctor! You can't think that he —," Ester
stopped, her face blanching at the thought.

"Shall not the Judge of all the earth do right?"
the doctor replied, then added: "Perhaps that one
eager word *pray* said as much to the ears of Him
whose thoughts are not as our thoughts as did that
old petition, 'Remember me when thou comest
into thy kingdom.' "

Ester never forgot that or the following day,
while the corpse of one she had known so well lay
in the house. She followed him to the quiet grave
and watched the red and yellow autumn leaves
float down around his coffin — dead leaves, dead
flowers, dead hopes, death everywhere. This was
not just a going-up higher, as Mr. Foster's death
had been; this was solemn and inexorable death.
More than ever she felt how impossible it was to
recall the days that had slipped away while she
slept and to undo now her neglected duties. She
had come for this, full of hope. Now one of those
whom she had met many times each day for years
and to whom she had never said the name of Jesus
was at this moment being lowered into his narrow
house. Although God had graciously given her a
moment of time and strength to use it, it was noth-

ing compared to those wasted years. She could
never know — at least until the call came for her,
whether or not at the eleventh hour this "poor man
cried, and the Lord heard him" and received him
into paradise.

Dr. Van Anden crossed over to Ester. He had
been watching her as she clasped her hands anxiously, the color drained from her face. "Ester, will
you and I ever again stand beside a newly made
grave, while it receives one whom we have known,
and have to settle with our consciences and our
Savior because we have not invited that one to
come to Jesus?"

And Ester avowed, "As that Savior hears me
and will help me, no, never again!"

CHAPTER XXII

LITTLE
PLUM PIES

ster was in the kitchen trimming off the puffy crusts of endless pies. She wore the old brown calico morning dress covered with the same huge bib apron that had journeyed through endless similar scrapes with her. Everything about her appeared to be exactly the same as three months ago. Yet as far as Ester and her future — and the future of everyone around her — were concerned, things were very different. Perhaps Sadie caught a glimmer of the peculiar change as she studied her sister curiously and noticed a new light in her eyes and a smoothness on the calm face. In fact, Sadie missed some wrinkles which she had supposed were part and parcel of Ester.

"How I did hate that part of it," she remarked, watching the fingers move deftly around each completed pie. "Mother said my edges always looked as if a mouse had marched around them nibbling all the way. My! How thoroughly I hate housekeeping. I pity the one who takes me for better or worse — always provided there exists such a poor victim on the face of the earth."

"I don't think you hate it half as much as you imagine," Ester answered kindly. "Anyway, you did nicely. Mother says you were a great comfort to her."

There was a sudden mist before Sadie's eyes. "Did Mother say that? The blessed woman — it takes so little to comfort her. Ester, I declare to you, if ever angels get into kitchens and pantries and the like, Mother is one of them. The way she endured my endless blunderings was perfectly angelic. I'm glad, though, that her day of martyrdom is over, and mine, too, for that matter."

Sadie had returned to the kingdom of spotless dresses and snowy cuffs and, above all, to the dear books and the academy. At that moment the academy bell sounded, and away she flitted.

Ester filled the oven with pies, then crossed to the side doorway to peep out at the glowing world. It was an ideal day; autumn meant to die in wondrous beauty that year. Ester folded her bare arms and gazed out upon the scene. She tingled with a new kind of restlessness this morning. She wanted to do something grand, something splendidly good. It was all very well to make good pies. Now they were being perfected in the oven, and she was waiting for something. If ever a girl longed for an occasion to show her colors, to honor her leader, it was Ester. Oh, yes, she meant to perform the next duty that came to her, but she ached to have that next duty be something grand, something that would show everyone what a new life she had embraced.

Dr. Van Anden was tramping about in his room over the side piazza, a very unusual activity for

him at that hour of the day. His windows were
open, and he was singing, and the fresh lake wind
carried the tune and words right down to Ester's
ear:

> I would not have the restless will
> That hurries to and fro,
> Seeking for some great thing to do,
> Or wondrous thing to know;
> I would be guided as a child,
> And led where'er I go.
>
> I ask thee for the daily strength,
> To none that ask denied,
> A mind to blend with outward life,
> While keeping at thy side;
> Content to fill a little space
> If thou be glorified.

Of course Dr. Van Anden did not know that Ester Ried stood in the doorway below and was at
that precise moment in need of just such help as
this. But what did that matter, as long as the Master knew?

Just then Ester's nose did its duty and alerted
her that the pies in the oven were burning. She ran
to their rescue, humming:

> Content to fill a little space
> If thou be glorified.

Eleven o'clock found her busily paring potatoes.
She was hurrying a little, for in spite of her nimble
fingers the work was getting the best of Maggie
and her, and one pair of very helpful hands was
missing.

Alfred and Julia appeared from somewhere in the outer regions, and Ester was too busy to see that they both wore rather woebegone expressions.

"Hasn't Mother gotten back yet?" queried Alfred.

"Why, no," said Ester. "She will not be back until tonight — perhaps not then. Didn't you know Mrs. Carleton was worse?"

Alfred kicked his heels against the kitchen door in a most dejected manner.

"Somebody's always sick," he grumbled. "A fellow might as well not have a mother. I never saw the beat — nobody for miles around here can have the toothache without borrowing Mother. I'm just sick and tired of it."

Ester had nearly laughed but catching a glimpse of the forlorn face, she thought better of it. "Something is awry now, I know. You never want Mother in such a hopeless way as that unless you're in trouble. So you see, you are just like the rest of them — everybody wants Mother when they are in any difficulty."

"But she is my mother, and I have a right to her, and the rest of 'em haven't."

"Well," said Ester soothingly, "suppose I be Mother this time. Tell me what's the matter, and I'll act as much like her as possible."

"You!" Alfred sniffed. "Odd work you'd make of it."

"Try me," was the good-natured reply.

"I ain't going to. I know well enough you'd say 'fiddlesticks' or 'nonsense' or some such word and finish up with 'Just get out of my way.' "

Ester's cheeks were pretty red over this exact imitation of her former, ungracious self, but she still answered energetically: "Very well, suppose I should make such a rude and unmotherlike reply — fiddlesticks and nonsense would not shoot you, would they?"

Alfred stopped kicking his heels against the door and laughed.

"Tell us all about it," continued Ester, following up her advantage.

"Nothing to tell, much, only all the folks are going sailing on the lake this afternoon and having a picnic in the grove, the very last one before snow. I meant to ask Mother to let us go, only how was I going to know that Mrs. Carleton would get sick and send someone all the way down here after her before daylight? I know she would have let me go, too. And they're going to take things, a basketful each one of 'em — and they wanted me to bring little bits of pies, like the ones Mother bakes in little round tins — you know, plum pies. She would have made me some, I know. She always does. But now she's gone, and it's all up, and I shall have to stay at home like I always do, just for sick folks. It's mean, anyhow."

Ester smothered a laugh over this curious jumble and asked humbly: "Is there really nothing that would do for your basket but little bits of plum pies?"

"No," Alfred explained earnestly. "Because, you see, they've got plenty of cake and such stuff. The girls bring that. And they do like my pies, awfully. I 'most always take 'em. Mr. Hammond likes them, too. He's going along to take care of us, and I shouldn't like to go without the little pies, because they depend upon them."

"Oh," said Ester, "girls go, too, do they?" And she looked for the first time at the long, sad face of Julia in the corner.

"Yes, and Jule is in just as much trouble as I am. They are all going to wear white dresses, and she's tore hers, and she says she can't wear it till it's ironed, 'cause it looks like a rope. Maggie says she can't and won't iron it today. Mother was going to mend it this very morning, and — oh, fudge! It's no use talking. We've got to stay at home, Jule, anyway." And the kicking heels commenced again.

Ester pared her last potato with a half-troubled, half-amused face. She was tired of baking for that day and felt like saying fiddlesticks to the little plum pies. And that white dress was torn criss-cross and every which way, and ironing was always hateful. Besides it did seem strange that when she wanted to do some great, nice thing, so many plum pies and torn dresses should step right into her path. Then unconsciously she repeated:

Content to fill a little space
If Thou be glorified.

Could He be glorified, though, by such very little things? Yet hadn't she wanted to influence Alfred and Julia for Him, and wasn't this her first opportunity? Besides, there was that verse: "Whatsoever thy hand findeth to do — ." At that point her thoughts formed into words.

"Well, sir, we'll see whether Mother is the only woman in this world after all. You tramp down to the cellar and bring me up that stone jar on the second shelf. We'll have those pies in the oven in a twinkling. And that little woman in the corner, with two tears rolling down her cheeks, may bring her white dress and my workbox and thimble and put two irons on the stove. My word for it — you shall both be ready by three o'clock, pies and all."

By three o'clock in the afternoon Ester was thoroughly exhausted, but little plum pies by the dozen were cuddling among snowy napkins in the willow basket.

Alfred's face was radiant. "You're just jolly, Ester! I didn't know you could be so good. Won't the boys chuckle over these pies, though? Ester, you even made seven more than Mother has ever made for me."

"Very well," replied Ester merrily, "then there will be seven more chuckles this time than usual."

Julia expressed her thoughts in a way more like her. She surveyed her skillfully mended, beautifully smooth white dress with smiling eyes. As Ester tied the blue sash in a dainty knot and stepped back to see that all was as it should be, she was suddenly confronted with this question: "Ester, what does make you so nice today? You didn't ever used to be so."

How Ester struggled with her desire to laugh or cry — she hardly knew which. These were little things she had done. It was shameful that, in all the years of her elder sisterhood, she had never before sacrificed even such a little bit of her own pleasure. Yet it was true, and it made her feel like crying. But the question had a ludicrous side — to think that all her beautiful plans for the day had culminated in plum pies and ironing.

She stooped and kissed Julia on her rosy cheek and answered gently, moved by some inward impulse: "I am trying to do all my work for Jesus nowadays."

"You didn't mend my dress and iron it and curl my hair and fix my sash for Him, did you?"

"Yes — every little thing."

"Why, I don't see how. I thought you did them

for me."

"I did, Julia, to please you and make you happy. But Jesus says that that is just the same as doing it for Him."

Julia's next question was very astute for one so young: "But, Ester, I thought you had been a member of the church a good many years. Sadie said so. Didn't you ever try to do things for Jesus before?"

Genuine shame burned across Ester's face and melted her heart. "No, I don't think I ever really did."

Julia wondered at her for a moment, then stood on tiptoe to return the kiss. "Well, I think it is nice, anyway. If Jesus likes to have you be so kind and take so much trouble for me, why, then, He must love me, and I mean to thank Him this very night when I say my prayers."

Ester rested for a moment in the armchair on the piazza and watched her little brother and sister scurrying off. She hummed again those two lines that had been making unconscious music in her heart all day:

> Content to fill a little space
> If Thou be glorified.

CHAPTER XXIII

CROSSES

he large church was full. There didn't seem to be space enough for another human being. People who were not given to visiting the house of God on a weeknight had certainly been drawn there this evening. Sadie Ried sat beside Ester in their mother's pew, and Harry Arnett, with a sober look on his boyish face, sat bolt upright at the end of the pew. Even Dr. Douglass leaned forward from the seat behind them and now and then addressed a word to Sadie.

They had been listening to such a sermon as was seldom heard — by that blessed man of God whose name was dear to hundreds and thousands of people. His hair was whitened with the frost of many years spent in the Master's service, and his voice and brain and heart were yet strong and powerful and "mighty through God." The Rev. Mr. Parker had been speaking to them. His theme was the soul, and his text: "What shall it profit a man if he gain the whole world and lose his own soul?"

Now the gray-haired veteran minister was leaning over the pulpit, waiting for the Christian witnesses to the truth of his solemn messages. A few earnest men, veterans too in the cause, gave their testimonies. Then one of those awful, disheartening, embarrassing pauses occurred that are encountered nowhere else on earth among intelligent men and women, who are given the liberty to talk, except in a prayer meeting! More silence, and still the aged servant stood with one arm resting on the Bible and looked down almost beseechingly upon that crowd of mute Christians.

"Ye are my witnesses, saith the Lord," he repeated in earnest tones.

Miserable witnesses they! Wasn't the Lord ashamed of them all, perhaps? Something like this flitted through Ester's brain as she surveyed that faithless company and noted here and there one who certainly ought to "take up his cross." Then some slight notion of the foolishness of that expression struck her. What a fearful cross it was, to be sure! How strange to use the same word in describing it that was used for that bloodstained, nail-pierced cross on Calvary.

Then a startling thought entered her mind. Was that cross borne only for men? Were they the only ones who could offer thanks because of Calvary? Surely her Savior hung there and bled and groaned and died for *her*. Why shouldn't she say, "By his stripes I am healed"? What if she did? What would people think? No, not that, either. What would Jesus think? That, after all, was the important question. Wasn't it possible that if she were to say in that assembled group, "I love Jesus," that Jesus, seeing her and hearing how her timid voice broke the awkward silence, would be greatly pleased?

She tried to imagine herself speaking to Him in her closet: "Dear Savior, I confess with shame that I have brought reproach upon Your name this day, for I said, in the presence of a great company of witnesses, that I loved You!" In defiance of her education and former belief upon this subject, Ester was obliged to confess, then and there, that this was all extremely ridiculous.

"Oh, well," said Satan, "it's not exactly wrong, of course. But then it isn't very modest or ladylike. And, besides, it is unnecessary. There are plenty of men to do the talking."

"But," said common sense, "I don't see why it's a bit more unladylike than the ladies' colloquy at the lyceum was last evening. More people were present than are here tonight. As for the men, they are perfectly mum. There seems to be plenty of opportunity for somebody."

"Well," said Satan, "it isn't customary at least, and people will think strangely of you. Doubtless it would do more harm than good."

This most potent argument, "People will think strangely of you," smothered common sense at once, as it is apt to do. Ester raised her head from the bowed position it had held during this whirl of thought and considered the question settled. Someone began to sing, and of all the words that could have been chosen, the most unfortunate ones for this decision came forth:

On my head He poured his blessing,
Long time ago;
Now He calls me to confess Him
Before I go.
My past life, all vile and hateful,
He saved from sin;

I should be the most ungrateful
Not to own Him.
Death and hell He bade defiance,
Bore cross and pain;
Shame my tongue this guilty silence
And speak His name.

This at once renewed the struggle, but in a different form. She no longer said, "Ought I?" but, "Can I?"

Still the silence seemed unbroken except for a voice here and there. Still Ester parleyed with her conscience, getting to the point of saying, When Mr. Harrison sits down, if there is another silence, I will try to say something. She did not quite mean, however, to do any such thing and proved her word false by remaining very still after Mr. Harrison sat down, although there was plenty of silence.

Then when Mr. Adams said a few words, Ester whispered the same assurance to herself, with exactly the same result. The opportunity to show the world just where she stood on this long-awaited decision had arrived at last, and this was how she was meeting it. Finally she knew by the pounding of her heart that the question was decided, that the very moment Deacon Graves sat down she would rise. Whether she would say anything or not would depend upon whether God gave her anything to say, but at least she could stand up for Jesus.

But Mr. Parker's voice followed that of Deacon Graves: "Am I to understand by your silence that there is not a Christian man or woman in all this company who has an unconverted friend he or she would like to have us pray for?"

Then the watching angel of the covenant came to

the aid of this trembling, struggling Ester. Such a sudden and overwhelming sense of longing for Sadie's conversion entered into her heart that all thought of what she would say and how she would say it and what people would think vanished entirely from her mind. Rising at once, she spoke clearly and earnestly: "Will you pray for a dear, dear friend?"

God sometimes uses humble means with which to break the spell of silence which Satan weaves around Christians. It was as if they had all suddenly awakened to a sense of their privileges.

Dr. Van Anden voiced his feelings: "I have a brother in the profession for whom I ask your prayers that he may become acquainted with the great Physician."

Request followed request for husbands and wives, mothers and fathers and children. Even timid Mrs. Ried murmured a request for her children who were out of Christ. And when at last Harry Arnett lifted his handsome boyish head from its bowed position and said in words that conveyed the sense of a decision, "Pray for me," the last film of pride disappeared. There are those living today who have reason never to forget that meeting.

"Is it your private opinion that our good doctor stirred up a streak of disinterested enthusiasm over my unworthy self this evening?" Dr. Douglass asked Sadie as they lingered on the piazza in the moonlight.

Sadie laughed. "I am sure I don't know. I'm prepared for anything strange that can possibly happen. Mother and Ester between them have turned the world upside down for me tonight. In case you are the happy man, I hope you are grateful."

"Extremely! I should be more so perhaps if people would be just to me in private and not so alarmingly generous in public."

"How bitter you are against Dr. Van Anden," Sadie said, observing the lowering brow and sarcastic curve of the lip. "How much I should like to know precisely what is the trouble between you!"

Dr. Douglass recovered his charm instantly. "Do I appear bitter? I beg your pardon for exhibiting so ungentlemanly a phase of human nature; yet hypocrisy does move me to — ," he stopped himself as he did whenever he was about to say something slightly discourteous.

"Just forget that last sentence," he added. "It was unwise and unkind. The trouble between us is not worthy of your thoughts. I wish I could forget it. I believe I could if he would allow me to."

At this particular moment the subject of the above conversation appeared in the door. Sadie gave a slight start. The possibility that Dr. Van Anden had heard the talk was not pleasant. She needn't have feared, for he had just come from his room and from his knees.

"Dr. Douglass, may I have a few words with you in private?" he asked a bit nervously.

"Certainly, if Miss Sadie will excuse us," Dr. Douglass replied graciously, though the tone said almost as plainly as words, To what do I owe this honor?

Dr. Van Anden led the way into the brightly lighted vacant parlor. Dr. Douglass stationed himself directly under the gaslight, where he could see the pale, anxious face of his companion clearly. He maintained an air of nonchalance and insolence.

Dr. Van Anden jumped into his subject: "Dr. Douglass, some years ago you did what you could

to injure me. Then I thought it was intentional.
Now I think that perhaps you did not mean to do
me harm and that you were sincere. Be that as it
may, I used language with you which I, as a Christian man, ought never to have used. I repented of it
long ago, but in my blindness I have never seen,
until this evening, that I ought to apologize to you
for it. God has shown me my duty. Dr. Douglass, I
ask your pardon for the angry words I spoke to
you that day."

The gentleman addressed continued to scruti-
nize Dr. Van Anden. He answered him icily: "You
are certainly very kind, now that your anger has
had time to cool during these intervening years, to
grant me the possibility of being sincere. Indeed I
was more Christian in my conclusions; I credited
you with being an honest blunderer. That I have
had occasion since to change my opinion is insignificant. But it would be more pleasant for both of
us if apologies could restore our friend, Mrs.
Lyons, to life."

During this response Dr. Van Anden's face had
passed through varying shades of anxiety, anger,
disgust and finally surprise. He sensed a new de-
velopment in the already complex matter, for he
asked a question evoked by Dr. Douglass's last
comment. "Do you think *I* administered that chlo-
roform?"

Dr. Douglass's cool composure seemed to melt
for a moment. "Who did?" he asked, eyes flashing.

"Dr. Gilbert."

"Dr. Gilbert?"

"Yes, sir."

"Why did I never know it?"

"I am sure I do not know." Dr. Van Anden wiped
his hand across his eyes wearily. "I had no idea

that you were not aware of it until this moment. It explains in part what was so mysterious to me. But even in that case, it would have been, as you said, a blunder, not a criminal act. However, we cannot undo that past. I desire, above all other things, to set myself right in your eyes as a Christian. I have probably been a stumbling-block to you. Only God knows how bitter the thought is. I have done wrong; I should have acknowledged it years ago. I can only do it now. Again I ask you, Dr. Douglass, will you pardon those bitter words I spoke to you?"

Dr. Douglass bowed stiffly, with increased arrogance visible in every line of his face. "Give yourself no uneasiness on that score, Dr. Van Anden, nor on any other, I beg you, as far as I am concerned. My opinion of Christianity is unusual perhaps, but it has not changed recently; nor is it likely to do so. Of course, every gentleman is bound to accept the apology of another, however late it may be offered. Shall I bid you good evening, sir?"

And with a low, dignified bow, Dr. Douglass returned to the piazza and Sadie. Dr. Van Anden groaned inwardly over his delay in attempting to set things right with Dr. Douglass. He retreated to his room and prayed that he might renew his zeal and his longing for the conversion of that man's soul.

"Have you been receiving a little fraternal advice?" inquired Sadie. Her mischievous eyes danced as she pictured the discomfiture of at least one of the two gentlemen — she didn't care which.

"Not at all. On the contrary, I've been giving a little of that commodity in a rather unpalatable form, I fear. I haven't a very high opinion of the world, Miss Sadie."

"Including yourself, do you mean?" Sadie replied demurely.

Dr. Douglass seemed annoyed at first, then he laughed. "Yes, including even such an important individual as I am. However, I have one quality I consider very rare — sincerity."

Both amused and puzzled, Sadie contemplated by moonlight the handsome form leaning against the pillar opposite her.

"I wonder, Dr. Douglass, if you are as sincere as you pretend to be. And I also wonder if the rest of the world is as much a set of humbugs as you believe? How do you think you escaped getting mixed up with the general humbuggism of the world? This Mr. Parker, now, talks as though he means what he says."

"He is a first-class fanatic of the most outrageous sort. There ought to be a law forbidding such ranters to carry on, on threat of imprisonment for life."

"Dr. Douglass," said Sadie, "I'd rather not hear you speak of that fine gentleman in such a way. He may be a fanatic and a ranter, but I believe he means it, and I can't help respecting him more than any cold-blooded moralist I ever met. Besides, I cannot forget that my honored father was among the despised class you speak of so scornfully."

"My dear friend," the doctor's tone softened at once, "forgive me if I have hurt you. It was not intentional. I don't know what I've been saying — unkind things perhaps, and that is always ungentlemanly. But I've been upset this evening, and that must be my apology. Pardon me for detaining you so long in the evening air. May I advise you professionally to go inside immediately?"

"May I advise you unselfishly to get into a better humor with the world in general — and Dr. Van Anden in particular — before you try to talk with a lady again?" Sadie answered with her usual banter; her dignified air had departed. "Meanwhile, if you would like to have free rein of this piazza to help you in stomping off your evil spirit, you shall be indulged. I'm going to the west side. The evening air and I are excellent friends." And with a feigned laugh and curtsy Sadie withdrew.

"I wonder," she asked herself aloud the moment she was alone, "I wonder what that man has been saying to him now? How unhappy these two gentlemen make themselves. It would be comforting to know right from wrong. I just wish I believed in everybody as I used to. The idea of this gray-headed minister being a hypocrite! That's absurd. But then the idea of Dr. Van Anden being what he is! Well, it's a strange world. I believe I'll go to bed."

CHAPTER XXIV

God's Way

r. Douglass was astonished and not a little disgusted with himself. As he marched up and down the long piazza, he tried to analyze his state of mind. He had always imagined himself to be a man who possessed keen powers of discernment. Yet at the same time he exercised considerable charity toward his errant fellowmen, was willing to overlook faults and mistakes and prided himself on the kind and gentlemanly way in which he could meet ruffled human nature of any sort. In fact, he kept himself on a pedestal and from its height looked calmly and apologetically down on weaker mortals.

But tonight he realized that his pedestal had crumbled, or he had tumbled from its height — at least *something* had happened. What had become of his powers of discernment? Here was this miserable doctor, who had been a thorn in his life; he had regarded him smugly as a pious hypocrite. Was he, after all, mistaken? The incident tonight made it appear that way. He had been deceived in the matter that had come between them years ago; he could see it plainly now. In spite of his attempt to shut it out, the doctor's earnest apology haunted him, demanding respect.

Now Dr. Douglass was honestly amazed at himself, because he was not pleased with this turn of events. Why wasn't he glad to discover that Dr. Van Anden was more of a man than he had assumed? This would certainly be consistent with the character of the courteous, unprejudiced gentleman he had considered himself to be up to now. But there was no avoiding the fact that the very thought of Dr. Van Anden irritated him, more so this evening than ever before. And the more he became convinced that he had blundered, the more irritated he became.

"Confound everybody!" he exclaimed at length in utter disgust. "Why on earth do I care about the contemptible whelp that I should waste my energy on him? What possessed the fellow to come whining to me tonight and set me off in such a miserable train of thought? I ought to have knocked him down for his insufferable impudence in dragging me out publicly in that meeting," he said aloud.

In his heart a quiet voice countered, "Oh, it's ridiculous for you to talk this way. You know perfectly well that Dr. Van Anden is not a contemptible whelp at all. He is a thoroughly educated, talented physician and a formidable rival. He didn't whine in the least this evening. He made an appropriate apology for what was not so very bad after all, and you half suspect yourself of admiring him."

"Fiddlesticks!" said Dr. Douglass aloud and stalked off to his room vowing to forget this troublesome evening.

The next two days seemed to be very busy to one member of the Ried household. Dr. Douglass sometimes appeared at meals and sometimes did not, but the parlor and the piazza were quite deserted, and even his own room saw little of him. By accident Sadie met him on the stairs and stopped to ask if the village was given over to smallpox or any other dire disease which required his constant attention.

"It is given over to madness," he retorted sharply and passed quickly by.

This encounter sent him on a long walk into the woods that very afternoon. In truth, Dr. Stephen Douglass was overcome with shock at his behavior. Two such days and nights as these last had been he hoped never to see again. His pet theories seemed to have deserted him without a moment's warning, and a spirit of darkness had taken up its abode in their place. Wherever he went, whatever he did, he was haunted by these new, strange thoughts. Sometimes he actually feared that he, at least, was losing his mind, whether or not the rest of the world was.

He did not believe in the power of prayer — and indeed knew nothing about it. He would have scoffed at the idea that Dr. Van Anden's constant, impassioned petitions had anything to do with him now. At the very time in which he was trudging through the dreary woods, kicking the red and yellow leaves from his path, Ester was in her little clothespress on her knees pleading with God for his soul and that through him Sadie might be reached. Had he known, he would have thought the whole scenario extremely funny.

After this long communion with himself he con-

cluded that he had worked too much and slept too
little; that his nerves were frazzled; and that he
was a fool to attend that abominable, sensational
meeting. The man actually had extraordinary
power over the common mind and used his elo-
quence to confuse an otherwise perfectly balanced
brain. It was no wonder, then, in his physically de-
pleted state, that his sympathetic mind should be
alarmed. So much for the disease; now for the rem-
edy. He would study less; at least he would stop
reading half the night away. He would begin to
practice some of his own preaching and learn to be
more systematic and more careful of this wonderful body that could cause so much suffering. He
would ride fast and long. Above all, he would keep
away from that church and that man with his
imaginary pictures and skillfully woven words.

Having determined his plan of action he felt better. There was no sense, he told himself, in yielding
to the sickly sentimentalism that had captivated
him for the past few days. He was ashamed of it
and would have no more of it. He was master of
his own mind, he guessed — always had been and
always would be. He started on his homeward
walk with a good deal of alacrity and much of his
usual composure.

But would the gracious Spirit which had been
struggling with him leave him indeed to himself?

"O God," pleaded Ester, "give me this one soul
in answer to my prayer. For the sake of Sadie, bring
this strong pillar obstructing her way to You. For
the sake of Jesus, who died for them both, bring
them both to yield to You."

Dr. Douglass paused at the place where the road
forked. He mused, and the subject of his musing
was no more important than this: Should he go

home by the river path or through the village? The
river path was longer, and it was growing late,
nearly teatime. But if he took the main road he
would pass his office where he was supposed to
be, as well as several houses where he ought to
have been, besides meeting several people along
the way whom he would rather not see just at present. He decided to take the river road and quick-
ened his pace quite in harmony with himself once
more and enjoying the autumn beauty spread
around him.

A little white speck attracted his attention. He
almost stopped to examine it, then smiled at his
curiosity and continued on. A bit of wastepaper
probably, he said to himself. Yet what a curious
shape it was — as if it had been carefully folded
and hidden under that stone. Suppose I see what it
is? Who knows but I shall find a fortune hidden in
it?

He turned back a step or two and reached down
for the little white speck. One corner of it was nestled under a stone. It was a ragged, rumpled,
muddy fragment of a letter or an essay which rain
and wind and water, it seemed, had done their best
to annihilate. Finally, becoming weary of their
plaything, those elements of nature had tossed it
contemptuously on the shore, and a pitying stone
had rolled down and covered and preserved a tiny
corner.

Dr. Douglass eyed it curiously, trying to deci-
pher the mud-stained lines. Being in a dreamy
mood he wondered what young, fair hand had
penned the words and what joy or sadness filled
them. Scarcely a word was legible, at least nothing
that would satisfy his curiosity, until he turned the
bit of paper, and the first line, which the stone had

hidden, shone out distinctly: "Sometimes I cannot help asking myself why I was made —." Here the corner was torn off, and whether that was the end of the original sentence or not, it was the end to him. God sometimes uses very simple means with which to confound the wisdom of this world.

Dr. Douglass did not stop to question strange thoughts nor why that bit of soiled, torn paper should gain so much power over him. He didn't even realize at the time that it was connected with his present confusion; he only knew that the foundation on which he had been building for years seemed suddenly to have been torn from under him by invisible hands. His feet were left to sink slowly down on nothing. And his soul embraced that solemn question with which he had never before troubled his logical brain: "I cannot help asking myself why I was made?" The paper held only one other legible word, turn it whichever way he would, and that word was "God." He shivered when he saw this, as if some awful voice had spoken it to his ear.

"What unaccountable force has taken possession of me?" he muttered at length. And swinging around he sat down on an old decaying log by the river and plunged into real, honest, solemn thought.

"Where is Dr. Douglass?" asked Julia, appearing at the dining room door just at teatime. "There's a boy at the door who says they want him at Judge Beldon's this very instant."

"He's nowhere," answered Sadie gravely, pausing in her task of arranging cups and saucers. "It's my private opinion that he has gone and hanged himself. He passed the window about one o'clock, looking precisely as I would picture a man who was about to commit that interesting act. Since then I've answered the bell seventeen times to give the same melancholy story of his whereabouts."

"My!" exclaimed the literal Julia, hurrying back to the boy at the door. She knew her sister well enough to have no faith in the hanging statement, but she honestly believed there were seventeen sick people waiting for the doctor.

The church was full again that evening. Sadie had at first declared herself unequal to another meeting that week but had finally allowed herself to be persuaded into going. She had nearly been the cause of poor Julia's disgrace because of the astonished look she affected when Dr. Douglass came down the aisle with his usual quiet manner. He took the seat directly in front of them.

The sermon was concluded. The text had been: "See I have set before thee this day life and good, death and evil." It seemed to some as if the aged servant of God had been given a glimpse of the two unseen worlds that wait for every soul and was painting from actual memory the picture for them to look upon. That most sobering of all hymns had just been sung:

There is a time, we know not when,
A point, we know not where,
That marks the destiny of men
'Twixt glory and despair.

There is a line, by us unseen,
That crosses every path,
The hidden boundary between
God's mercy and His wrath.

Silence had all but fairly settled on the waiting

congregation when a strong, firm voice broke in upon it. "I believe in my soul that I have met that point and crossed that line this day. I surely met God's mercy and His wrath face-to-face and struggled in their power. Your hymn says, 'To cross that boundary is to die,' but I thank God there are two sides to it. I feel that I have been standing on the very line, that my feet had nearly slipped. Tonight I step over onto mercy's side. From now on count me among those who have chosen life."

"Amen," said the visiting minister with a radiant face.

"Thank God," said the earnest pastor with emotion.

Two heads bowed in the silent ecstasy of prayer — Ester's and Dr. Philip Van Anden's. As for Sadie, she sat as straight and still as if she had been petrified with amazement: the strong, firm voice belonged to Dr. Stephen Douglass!

An hour later Dr. Van Anden was pacing excitedly up and down the long parlor, waiting for he hardly knew what, when a shadow fell between him and the gaslight. He glanced up to see Dr. Douglass, who was standing precisely where he had when they had met there before. Dr. Van Anden stepped forward, and the two gentlemen clasped hands tightly.

Dr. Douglass broke the poignant silence first: "Doctor, will you forgive all the past?"

"My brother in Christ!" was Dr. Van Anden's heartfelt reply.

As for Ester, she prayed in her clothespress with thanksgiving for Dr. Douglass and with more hope for Sadie. She didn't know that a corner of the poor little letter that had slipped from Julia's hand and floated down the stream one summer morning, causing her such a miserable, miserable day, was lying at that moment in Dr. Douglass's notebook. Nor did she know that he counted it as the most precious of all his treasured bits of paper. Indeed, "His ways are not as our ways."

CHAPTER XXV

SADIE SURROUNDED

h," said Sadie, tossing her brown curls merrily, "please don't waste any more precious breath on me. I'm an unfortunate case, not worth struggling for. Just let me have a few hours of peace. If you'll promise not to say 'meeting' again to me, I'll promise not to laugh at you once after this long drawn-out spasm of goodness has quieted, and you have each descended to your usual level once more."

"Sadie!" exclaimed Ester. "Do you think we are all hypocrites and don't mean a bit of this?"

"By no means, my dear sister of charity, at least not all of you. I'm a firm believer in diseases of all sorts. This is one of those violent, highly contagious diseases; they must run their course, you know. I haven't lived in the house with two learned physicians all this time without learning that fact, but I consider this to be almost at its height. I'm living in hourly expectation of the 'turn.' But, my dear, I don't think you need to worry about me in the least. I don't believe I'm a fit subject for such trouble. You know I never took whooping cough or measles, though I have been exposed to them a great many times."

"Don't, Sadie, please," Ester implored.

Seeing her sister's pale, anxious face, Sadie sobered at once. "Ester," she said quietly, "I don't think you are playing games. I don't, positively. You are thoroughly in earnest. I think you've been through some very hard times lately, what with sickness and watching and death, and your nerves are completely unstrung. I don't wonder at your feelings, but you'll get over it in a little while and be yourself again."

"Oh," said Ester tremulously, "I pray God I may never be myself again — not the old self you mean."

"You will," Sadie answered. "Things will go haywire — the fire won't burn, the kettle won't boil, and the milk pitcher will tip over. All sorts of mischievous things will keep on happening after a little bit, just as usual, and you will feel like smashing up everything in spite of all these meetings."

Ester sighed. The old difficulty again — things would not be undone. The weeds she had sown carelessly during all these years had taken deep root and would not let go.

"Sadie, answer me just one question. What do you think of Dr. Douglass?"

Sadie's face darkened. "Never mind what I think of him," she retorted and left the room abruptly.

What she thought of him was: He had become what he had pretended to consider the most despicable thing on earth — a hypocrite. Sadie, of course, had no personal knowledge of the power of the Spirit of God over a human soul. She had no concept of how so mighty a change could be wrought in Dr. Douglass in the space of a few hours; therefore her only solution to the mystery was to achieve the end she thought he had in mind. Dr. Douglass had chosen to assume a new character.

Later, on that same day, Sadie encountered Dr. Douglass. Rather she went to the side piazza ready for a walk, and he approached her eagerly from the west end.

"Miss Sadie, I've been waiting for you. I have a few words that I *must* say."

"Proceed," said Sadie, folding her hands demurely in front of her and feigning seriousness.

"I want to do justice at this late day to Dr. Van Anden. I misjudged him, wronged him and perhaps prejudiced you against him. I want to undo my work."

"Some things can be done more easily than they can be undone," Sadie replied. "You certainly have done your best to prejudice me not only against Dr. Van Anden, but also against all other persons who hold his views. And you have succeeded splendidly. I congratulate you."

A pained expression that she had seen once or twice on his face crossed it now. "I know — I have been blind and stupid, wicked, anything you will. I regret it now most bitterly, and I am most eager to make amends."

"What a capital actor you would make, Dr. Douglass. Are you sure you haven't mistaken your vocation?"

"I know what you think of me," he acknowledged in a humble way unlike any she had heard from him before. "You think I am playing a part.

Though what my motive could be I cannot imagine, can you? But I assure you that, if ever I was sincere in anything in all my life, I am now about this matter."

"There is a most unfortunate 'if' in the way, doctor. The trouble is, I have very serious doubts as to whether you ever were sincere about anything in your life. As to motives, the world is full of power-hungry people. Everyone wants to influence someone. Aren't you satisfied with what you've accomplished in me? You will observe that 'I have a very poor opinion of the world.' "

The doctor did not notice the quotation of his favorite expression but answered with a touch of his usual dignity: "I may have deserved this treatment at your hands, Miss Sadie. No doubt I have, although I am not aware of saying anything to you that I didn't think I meant. I've been a fool. I am willing — yes, and eager to admit it. But there are surely some among your friends whom you can trust if you cannot me. I — "

Sadie interrupted him. "For instance, that 'first-class fanatic of the most objectionable stamp,' the man you thought, not three days ago, ought to be bound by law to keep the peace. I suppose you would have me unhesitatingly believe every word he says?"

Dr. Douglass's face brightened instantly. "I remember those words, Miss Sadie, and how honestly I spoke them — and how bitterly I felt when I spoke them. My surest proof that this thing is of God is the wonderful change that has come in my feelings for that blessed man. I pray that God will let him speak to your soul in the same way that he has to mine. Oh, Sadie, I have led you astray. May I not help you back?"

"I'm not a weather vane, Dr. Douglass, to be whirled about by every expedient wind. Besides, I'm familiar with one verse in the Bible which you don't seem to have heard of: 'Whatsoever a man soweth, that shall he also reap.' You have sowed well and faithfully; be content with your harvest."

I don't know what the pale lips would have answered to this mocking spirit. At that moment Dr. Van Anden and the black ponies spun around the corner and halted before the gate.

"Sadie," said the doctor, "are you in the mood for a ride? I have five miles to drive."

"Dr. Van Anden," returned Sadie, "the last time you and I took a ride together we quarreled."

"Precisely," said the doctor, apologetically. "Let's take another now and make up."

"Very well," she laughed, and they were off.

For the first mile or two he kept a tight rein and let the ponies skim over the ground. They talked very little. After that he slackened his speed and leaned back in the carriage. "Now we are ready to make up."

"How shall we begin?" asked Sadie gravely.

"Who quarreled?" answered the doctor.

"Well," said Sadie, "I understand what you are waiting for. You think I was very rude and unladylike in my replies to you during that last interesting ride we took. You think I jumped to the wrong conclusions and used some unnecessarily sharp words. I think so myself, and if it will be of any use to you to know it, I don't mind telling you in the least."

"That is a very excellent beginning," admitted the doctor heartily. "I think we'll have no difficulty in settling the matter. For my part, it won't sound as good as yours. However much I blundered in what I said, I said it honestly, in good faith, and with a good and pure motive. But I can say with equal honesty that I was overly concerned and that Dr. Douglass was never worthy of such little regard as I imagined him to be. Nothing could have made me happier than the noble stand he has recently taken. Indeed I feel honored by his acquaintance."

"A mutual admiration society," laughed Sadie sarcastically. "Did you and Dr. Douglass have a private rehearsal? You interrupted him in a similar rhapsody over your perfections."

Instead of being annoyed, Dr. Van Anden's face glowed with pleasure.

"Did he explain our misunderstanding too?" he asked eagerly. "That was very good of him."

"Of course. He is the soul of nobility — a villain yesterday and a saint today. I don't understand such marvelously rapid changes, doctor."

"I know you don't," the doctor answered quietly. "Although you have exaggerated both terms, a great and marvelous change has occurred, which must be experienced to be understood. Will you ever seek it for yourself, Sadie?"

"Probably not, since I very much doubt that any such phenomenon exists."

Dr. Van Anden showed no surprise at her response but answered her steadily. "Oh, no, you don't doubt it in the least. Don't try to make yourself out to be that most unreasonable creature — someone who doesn't believe in what is as clear to a thinking mind as the sun is at noonday. We don't need to argue about this. You have seen some foolish, inconsistent deeds by many who call themselves Christians. You suppose they have shaken your belief in the truth of the thing itself. But that's

not true. Your dear father lived and died in the
faith. You no more doubt that he is in heaven today, brought there by the power of the Savior he
trusted, than you doubt your own existence at this
moment."

Dr. Van Anden was the one person who could
subdue Sadie to the point of silence, a rare thing
for her, but in her inmost heart she felt his words to
be true. That dear, dear father's life had been one
long evidence to the truth of the religion he professed. Yes, it was so. She no more doubted he was
at this moment in that blessed heaven he had constantly hoped for than she doubted the shining of
the sun. He, being dead, yet spoke to her. Besides,
Sadie had of late begun to believe that Dr. Van Anden lived a life that just might stand up under her
kind of scrutiny — a true, earnest, courageous life.
He was a man not likely to be deceived.

Sitting back in the carriage nonchalantly, she allowed herself to be convinced that, however most
people lived and believed, there was always her
father — safe, safe in the Christian's heaven. Besides him Sadie actually knew of a few, a very few,
she thought — who were still living and were
heading for that same distant place. Sadie had
stood upon the brink and was yet standing there;
but reason and the long-buried father kept her
from toppling over into the chasm of settled unbe-
lief. "Blessed are the dead which die in the Lord
from henceforth: Yea, saith the Spirit, that they
may rest from their labors; and their works do follow them."

But something must be said. Sadie was not going to sit there and let Dr. Van Anden think she was
conquered; she'd rather quarrel with him than
have that. He had espoused Dr. Douglass's cause

so emphatically — let him argue for him now.
There was nothing like a good sharp argument to
lessen the effect of unpleasant personal questions.
She blazed into sudden indignation: "I think Dr.
Douglass is a hypocrite!"

"Very well. What then?"

Sadie had no answer.

"Mr. Smith is a drunkard," Dr. Van Anden continued, "therefore I will be a thief. Is that Miss
Sadie Ried's logic?"

"I don't see the point."

"Don't you? Wasn't that remark about Dr.
Douglass a way to hide behind the supposed sin of
another — an excuse for you not to be a Christian,
because somebody else pretended to be? Is that
sound logic, Sadie? When your next classmate
peeps in her book during a test and thereby dis-
graces herself and becomes a hypocrite, do you
promptly declare that you will not study anymore?
It's fashionable in talking about religion to point
out the shortcomings and inconsistencies of others
and try to use them as a cover for our own sins. But
that's ridiculous, after all. You won't see it prac-
ticed when any other subject is discussed."

Clearly, Sadie must respond in a common-sense
way with this straightforward man, if she was to
talk at all. She resolved to say for once just what
she meant and raised her eyes to meet the doctor's.
"I think about these things sometimes, doctor. A lot
of it seems to be humbug. Some are sincere, and
there is a right way. I have been tempted many
times during the last few weeks to discover for myself the secret of power in the life of a Christian.
But certain considerations, which you'd think are
ridiculous, always stop me — not to mention the
absurd inconsistency of others."

"Would you mind telling me some of the considerations?"

As soon as Sadie began to talk honestly, the doctor lost his cool indifference and expressed a kind, thoughtful interest.

"No," she hesitated, "I don't know that I mind, but you won't understand them. For instance, if I were a Christian I'd have to give up one of my favorite amusements — dancing. It is almost a passion with me, and I am not ready to give it up."

"Why should you feel obliged to do so if you were a Christian?"

Sadie gave him a long searching look. "Do you think Christians should dance?" she asked finally.

"I haven't said what I think on the subject, but I feel sure that it is not the question for you to decide right now. First settle the all-important one of your personal acceptance of Christ. Then the time will come to decide the other matter, for or against, as your conscience may dictate."

"Oh, but," said Sadie positively, "I know very well what my conscience would dictate, and I am not ready for it."

"Isn't dancing an innocent amusement?"

"For me, yes, but not for a Christian," Sadie acknowledged, then asked abruptly: "Don't you think there should be a difference between Christians and those who are not?"

"Yes, I do. Do you think every person should or shouldn't be a Christian?" the doctor asked.

Sadie was silent again. After a moment she spoke, this time haughtily. "I think you understand what I mean, doctor, though you wouldn't admit it for the world. I don't suppose I feel very deeply on the subject, or else I would not offer such a trivial excuse. But this is honestly where I am. Whenever

I think about religion at all, this question comes up. It would be foolish for me to argue against dancing, for I don't know — or care — much about the arguments. But I do know this: that a distinct inconsistency lies between a profession of religion and dancing. Usually those who make no such profession see it. The others don't seem as able to see it. Most of us, however, laugh a little over dancing Christians. Whether this is an actual inconsistency or simply a foolish prejudice on our part, I've never taken the trouble to find out. It's enough for me that it's true.

"If I were an honest believer in that religion which leads one of its teachers to say that he will eat no meat while the world stands if it makes his brother to offend, I would give up my dancing. But since I'm not, I see no harm in my favorite amusement and am not ready to give it up; and that is what I mean by its being innocent for me and not innocent for professing Christians."

Dr. Van Anden seemed to have grown weary of the whole subject. He leaned back in his carriage and let the reins fall. Then he reached over and coolly took one of Sadie's small gloved hands in his own. "Sadie, would you let me put my arm around you?"

Sadie withdrew her hand instantly and sat bolt upright. In the iciest of tones she exclaimed, "Dr. Van Anden!"

"Just what I expected," returned that gentleman, looking with satisfaction on his angry companion. "Sadie, please forgive my obtuseness. If it's proper and courteous and all that sort of thing, I just can't see why I, a friend of long standing, shouldn't enjoy the same privilege — that of putting my arm around you — that you give Fred Kenmore. You were introduced to him only last week, and I heard you say you have danced with him five times."

Sadie looked confused and annoyed, but finally she laughed, for lack of anything better to do under the present circumstances.

"That's what puzzles me," continued the doctor. "I don't understand how refined young ladies can permit relative strangers to pay them certain kinds of attention which, in other situations, they repel. Won't you think about the seeming inconsistency a little? It's the only suggestion I wish to offer on the question now. When you have settled that other most important matter, this thing will presently fall into place for you. Meanwhile, this is the house where I must call. Will you hold my horses, Miss Sadie, while I see to matters inside?"

CHAPTER XXVI

CONFUSION, CROSS-BEAR-
ING AND CONSEQUENCE

ne morning it rained, not a soft, silent, warm rain, but a gusty, windy,
turbulent one — a rain that poured
into slightly raised windows and
hurled itself angrily into your face
whenever you ventured to open a door. It was a
day in which fires didn't like to burn but smol-
dered and sizzled and smoked. People walked
around shivering, their shoulders shrugged up under little dingy, unbecoming shawls, and the
clouds were low and gray and heavy. Everything
and everybody seemed generally out of sorts.

Ester was no exception. A toothache had kept
her awake during the night, and one cheek was
swollen in the morning. One tooth still snarled
threateningly whenever the slightest whisper of a
draft came to it. The exalted views of life and duty
which had influenced her so much during the past
few weeks seemed to have deserted her. In short,
her body had gained that mortifying ascendancy
over the soul which it sometimes accomplishes. All

her hopes and enthusiasms seemed blotted out.

Things in the kitchen were uncomfortable. Maggie had seized on this occasion for having the mumps and, on the advice of her sympathizing mistress, had pinned a hot flannel around her face and gone to bed. The same unselfish counsel had been given to Ester, but she had just enough grace left to refuse to desert the camp. Dinner had to be ready for twenty-four people in spite of nerves and teeth. But just here the supply of grace failed her, and she worked in ominous gloom.

Julia had been pressed into service and was stoning raisins — or eating them (a close observer would have found it difficult to discover which). She was certainly rasping the nerves of her sister in those unnumbered ways that a thoughtless, restless, inquisitive child has for distracting a troubled brain. Ester endured with what patience she could the unceasing demands upon her and worked at the interminable cookies with commendable zeal. Alfred entered with a bang and a whistle and held open the side door while he talked. In rushed the spiteful wind, and all the teeth in sympathy with the aching one set up an immediate growl.

"Mother, I don't see any. Why, where is Mother?" questioned Alfred.

"Shut that door!"

"Well, but," said Alfred, "I want Mother. I say, Ester, will you give me a cookie?"

"No!" exclaimed Ester. "Did you hear me tell you to shut that door this instant?"

"Well, now, don't bite a fellow." Alfred looked curiously at his sister. The door closed with a heavy bang. "Mother! Say, Mother," he continued, as his mother emerged from the pantry, "I don't see anything of that hammer. I've looked everywhere.

Mother, can't I have one of Ester's cookies? I'm awful hungry."

"Why, I guess so, if you are really suffering. Try again for the hammer, my boy. Don't let a poor little hammer get the better of you."

"Well," said Alfred, "I won't." Seizing a cookie he bestowed a triumphant look upon Ester and a loving one upon his mother and vanished amid a renewal of the whistle and bang.

This little scene did not help Ester. She rolled away vigorously at the dough, feeling disturbed and outraged. Finally she let out her emotions. "Julia, don't eat another raisin. You've gotten away with about half of them now."

Julia looked aggrieved. "Mother lets me eat raisins when I pick them over for her."

"Keep your elbows off the table."

Silence reigned while the work continued. Soon Julia recovered her composure. "Say, Ester, what makes you prick little holes all over your biscuits?"

"To make them rise better."

"Does everything rise better after it is pricked?"

Sadie was paring apples at the end table and interposed: "If you find that to be the case, Julia, you must be very careful after this, or we shall have Ester pricking you when you don't 'rise' in time for breakfast in the morning."

Julia suspected she was being teased and appealed to her older sister: "Honestly, Ester, do you prick them so they will rise better?"

"Of course. I told you so, didn't I?"

"Well, but why does that help them any? Can't they get up unless you make holes in them, and what is the whole reason for it?"

Now these were not easy questions to answer, especially for a girl with a toothache, and Ester's answer was not much to the point.

"Julia, I declare — you are enough to distract one. If you ask any more questions I will certainly send you upstairs out of the way."

Her scientific investigations thus nipped in the bud, Julia returned again to silence and raisins, until the vigorous beating of some eggs roused anew the spirit of inquiry. "Say, Ester, please tell me why the whites all foam and get thick when you stir them, just like beautiful white soapsuds." She rested her elbow, covered with its blue sleeve, plump into the platter containing the beaten yolks.

You must remember Ester's toothache; but even then I regret to say that this disaster culminated in a decided box on the ear for poor Julia and in her being sent weeping upstairs.

Sadie looked up with a satisfied laugh in her eyes. "You didn't keep your promise, Ester, and let me live in peace, so I needn't keep mine. I consider you pretty well out of the spasm which has lasted for so many days."

"Sadie, I am really ashamed of you." Mrs. Ried shook her head, then added kindly: "Ester, poor child, I wish you would wrap your face in something warm and lie down awhile. I am afraid you are suffering a great deal."

Poor Ester! It had been a hard day. Late in the afternoon she stood at the table and cut the bread, cake, cheese and cold meat for tea. When the sun had made a rift in the clouds and was peeping in to say good night; when the throbbing nerves had grown quiet once more, she thought back upon this weary day in shame and pain. How very little her valiant resolves and efforts had been worth after all. How far back she seemed to have slipped in that one day — without enough strength to bear even the little trials that befell an ordinarily quiet life! How she had lost the recent influence over Alfred and Julia by a few cross words! How much reason she had given Sadie to think that her attempts at following the Master were, after all, only spasmodic and idealistic!

But Ester had visited that little clothespress upstairs in search of help and forgiveness, and now she clearly saw there was something to do besides mourn over her failures. It was hard to do it, too. Ester had a proud spirit, and it was very humbling to confess that she was in the wrong. She shrank from the task, until she finally grew ashamed of herself for that. At last, without giving her resolve time to falter, she called to the twins, who were occupying seats in one of the dining-room windows and whispering soberly to each other.

"Children, come here a moment, will you?"

The two had been very shy of Ester since the morning's trials and were at that moment sympathizing with each other in a manner uncomplimentary to her. However, they slid down from their perch and responded slowly to her call.

Ester glanced up as they entered the storeroom and then went on cutting her cheese, but spoke to them gently: "I want to tell you both how sorry I am that I spoke so crossly and unkindly to you this morning. It was very wrong of me. I thought I never would displease Jesus in that way again, but I did, you see. And now I am very sorry indeed, and I want you to forgive me."

Alfred looked aghast. This was an Ester he had never seen before, and he didn't know what to say. He wriggled the toes of his boots together and scrutinized them in bewilderment. At last he stammered: "I didn't know your cheek ached till

Mother told me, or else I'd have shut the door right straight away. I ought to have anyhow, cheek or no cheek."

This last he mumbled with more scrutinizing of his boots. It was a new endeavor for Alfred — voluntarily admitting that he was in the wrong.

Julia burst forth. "And I was very careless and naughty to keep putting my elbows on the table after you had told me not to, and I am ever so sorry that I made such a lot of trouble for you."

"Well, then," said Ester, "we'll all forgive each other, shall we, and begin over again? And, children, I want you to understand that I am trying to please Jesus. And when I fail, it is because of my own wicked heart. I am so eager for you to love this same Jesus now, while you are young, and get Him to help you."

Their mother called the children at this moment, and Ester dismissed them each with a kiss. There was a little rustle in the flour room. Sadie, whom nobody knew was downstairs, emerged from the room with suspiciously red eyes but a laughing face. "Ester," said she, "I'm positively afraid that you are growing into a saint, and I know that I'm a sinner. I consider myself mistaken about the spasm — it is evidently a settled disease."

While the bell tolled for evening service, Ester stood in the front doorway and peered doubtfully up and down the damp pavements and muddy streets and felt of her swollen cheek. How much she seemed to need the rest and help of God's house tonight, and yet —

Julia's little hand stole softly into hers. "We've been talking about what you said you wanted us to do, Alfred and I. We've talked about it a good deal lately. We 'most wish so, too."

Before Ester could reply other than by grasping the small hand, Dr. Douglass appeared. His horses and carriage were waiting.

"Miss Ried," he said, pausing with his foot on the carriage step and finally turning back, "I am driving down to church this evening. I have a call to make afterward. Will you ride down with me? I would especially enjoy your company. Besides, it is much too unpleasant for walking."

Ester's face flushed a rosy pink at the thought. "I'm so glad. I did want to go to church tonight, and I was afraid it would be unwise on account of my tooth."

Alfred and Julia sat in front of them in church. Ester watched them with a prayerful, but troubled heart. What right had she to expect an answer to her petitions when her life had been working against them all that day? And yet the blood of Christ was all-powerful, and there was always His righteousness to plead. She bent her head in re-newed supplications for these two. "And it shall come to pass, that before they call I will answer, and while they are yet speaking I will hear."

Into one of the breathless stillnesses, while beat-ing hearts awaited the requests they hoped would be made, Julia's trembling, yet clear voice broke: "Please pray for me."

There was a little choking in Alfred's throat and a good deal of shuffling with his boots. It was so much more of a struggle for the rugged little boy than for the gentle little girl. But he stood coura-geously to his feet at last. His words, though few, were distinct and emphatic and full of as much meaning as any which had been spoken there that evening.

"Me, too."

CHAPTER XXVII

THE TIME
TO SLEEP

ife scooted busily along. At the end of December the blessed daily meetings concluded; that is, they closed with the first week of the new year, which the church kept as a sort of jubilee week to honor the glorious things that had been done for them.

The new year opened in joy for Ester. Many things had changed. The honest, straightforward little Julia transferred all her energy into this new life which had occupied her soul, and the strong brother had too determined a nature to do anything halfway, so Ester was sure of this young sister and brother. Her relationship with her mother was different too. They had each discovered that the other was bound on the same journey and that delightful resting places occurred along the way.

Ester herself was slowly but surely maturing. Little crosses that she stooped and faithfully picked up became fewer and fewer, and some of them developed into positive pleasures. Many things cast rays of light all about her path and into her heart.

One sorrow lingered. Sadie slid giddily on her downward way. If she seemed to have a serious thought at night, it vanished with the next morning's sunshine, and day by day Ester realized more fully how many tares the enemy had sown while she was sleeping. Sometimes the burden grew almost too heavy to bear, and again she would take heart and renew her efforts and her prayers with fervor.

It was about this time that Ester noticed a new feeling. She was not sick exactly, and yet not quite well. She discovered, much to her surprise, that she was in the habit of sitting down on a stair to rest before she had reached the top of the first flight. Furthermore, she was sometimes forced to stop her sweeping and clap her hands suddenly over a strange beating in her heart. She laughed at her mother's anxious face and pronounced herself quite well indeed, only perhaps a little tired.

Meanwhile, she planned all sorts of ways to be useful. She could not go away on a mission because her mission had come to her. For one thing she realized her mother needed her. She took up the work that lay around her bravely and eagerly, but her restless spirit craved more. She must do something for the Master outside this narrow circle.

One evening her enthusiasm reached a new height; it had been fed for several days on a new project that was starting in the town. Afterward Ester remembered every little incident connected with that evening: the family sitting room seemed so cozy with her as its only occupant. The coals glowed in the open grate. They flashed such a brilliant color over the crimson-cushioned rocker in which she sat. She was writing Abbie a letter, full of excited dreams for busy, bright work. "I'm surprised that I ever thought there was nothing worth living for," she wrote. "Why life isn't half long enough for the things that I want to do. I am so eager to get to work." She stopped when she heard Dr. Van Anden's step in the hall and dashed out to speak with him.

"Doctor, are you in a hurry? Have you just five minutes for me?"

"Ten," smiled the doctor, stepping into the cheery little room.

Ester plunged at once into her subject, not even waiting to offer him a seat. "Aren't you the chairman of that committee to obtain teachers for the evening school?"

"I am."

"Have you all the help you want?"

"Not by any means. Volunteers to teach factory girls are not easy to find."

"Well, doctor, do you think — would you be willing to suggest my name as one of the teachers? I would so like to be included."

To her dismay Dr. Van Anden's face clouded. He shook his head. "I don't think I can, Ester."

Amazed and hurt, Ester said nothing for a moment. "It's no matter," she said at last. "Of course I know little about teaching and perhaps could not do any good. But I thought, if help was scarce, you might — well, never mind."

"It's not that, Ester," he admitted, the lines deepening on his face. "We would be glad of your help," he paused and walked over to the fireplace, resting his hand on the mantel and staring into the sizzling coals. Then he turned to her. "I don't know how to tell you, Ester."

"Why, doctor, you don't need to tell me anything," Ester said sharply. "I'm not a child who
must have the truth sugarcoated. If my help is not
needed, that's sufficient."

"Your help is exactly what we need, Ester, but
your health is not sufficient for the work."

Ester laughed. "Why, doctor, what an absurd
idea. In a week I shall be as well as ever. If that is
all, you may surely count me as one of your teachers."

The doctor smiled slightly and then asked:
"Don't you wonder what is causing this strange
fatigue that is creeping over you — and the sudden
flutterings of your heart, along with the pain and
faintness, which overtake you without warning?"

Ester's face paled, but she asked quietly: "How
do you know all this?"

"Your mother, Dr. Douglass and others close to
you have seen the change. Of course, I can't be
sure. But I am a physician, Ester. Do you think it is
kind to keep a friend in the dark about what very
much concerns him, simply to spare his feelings
for a little while?"

"Why, Dr. Van Anden, you don't think, you
don't mean that — please tell me exactly what you
mean."

Perhaps the doctor's silence answered her or
perhaps her own heart told her the secret, for a
sudden gray pallor spread over her face. For an
instant the room darkened and whirled around
her. She staggered as if she might fall, then caught
hold of the little red rocker and sank into it. Leaning both elbows on the writing table before her, she
buried her face in her hands.

Later Ester recalled the strange thoughts which

spun around in her head. Life in all the various stages she had hoped to experience; all the endless plans she had made; all the things she had meant to do and be, came and stared her in the face. Nowhere did her dreams cross with death; she had never planned for that. Was He to come for her so soon, before any of these things were accomplished? Must she leave Sadie — bright, cheerful, unsafe Sadie — and go where she could not work for her anymore?

Then, like a picture laid out before her, that day on the train, on her way to New York, returned to her: the Christian stranger, who was no longer a stranger but her friend and was in heaven; the old woman with her kind face and that strange sentence on her lips: "Maybe my coffin will do it better than I can." Well, maybe her coffin could do it for Sadie. Oh, the blessed thought!

Plans? Yes, but perhaps God had plans, too. What did hers matter compared to His? If He wanted her to finish her earthly work by lying down soon in the unbroken calm of the "rest that remaineth," what was that to her?

"Are you certain?" she asked without raising her head. "Do you know when it will happen?"

"That last we cannot tell, dear friend. You may be with us for years yet, or it may come suddenly. I think it's a grievous error to treat a Christian woman like a child. I wanted to tell you before the shock would be harmful to you."

"I understand."

She hesitated. "Does Dr. Douglass agree with you?"

The speed with which he answered and the pain in his voice showed her he was anticipating her question. "Dr. Douglass will not *let* himself believe it."

A long silence fell between them. Dr. Van Anden stood there, leaning against the mantel. Never for a moment did he turn his eyes away from that motionless figure before him.

Only the loving, compassionate Savior knew what was passing in that young heart.

At last Ester arose and drew near to the doctor. "Dr. Van Anden, I am so much obliged to you." Sweetness played about her mouth, and a strange calm rested in her voice. "Don't be afraid to leave me now. I think I need to be alone."

He felt that all words were useless now and bowed silently, softly letting himself out of the room.

Immediately Ester turned to the table. There lay the letter in which she had been writing those last words: "Why, life isn't half long enough for the things that I want to do." She picked up the letter quietly and dispatched it to the glowing coals upon the grate. Her mood had changed.

Slowly and surely, as such bitter things do steal in upon a family, it became known that Ester was an invalid. Little by little her duties narrowed; one by one her various plans were relinquished. The dear mother first, and then Sadie, and finally the children grew accustomed to watching her footsteps and saving her from the stairs, from the lifting, from every possible burden. At first only rarely and then, as the weeks passed, more frequently, she did not get down further than the little sitting room but was settled amid pillows on the couch, "enjoying poor health," as she humorously phrased it.

Softly and stealthily the shadow crept in, until June came and brought roses and Cousin Abbie.

Ester received her in her own room, propped among the pillows in her bed.

Gradually they became used to that also, as God in His infinite mercy had planned that human hearts shall grow used to the inevitable. They even told each other hopefully that the warm weather was what depressed her so much and that as the summer heat cooled into autumn she would grow stronger. And she had radiant days in which she really seemed to grow strong; those days deceived everyone except Dr. Van Anden and her.

During one of those good days Sadie came home from school full of a new idea. She curled herself in front of Ester's couch to amuse her with it.

"Mr. Hammond's last — such a curious idea, as like him as possible, and like nobody else. Our class will graduate in just two years from this time, and there are fourteen of us, an even number, which is lucky for Mr. Hammond. Well, we are each, don't you think, to write a letter. It's to be as sensible, honest and exciting as we can make it and as historic, sentimental, poetic or otherwise as we please. But it must truly represent our views. Then we are to make a grand exchange of letters among the class. The young lady who receives my letter, for instance, is to keep it sealed and under lock and key until graduation day. Then it is to be read before everyone — scholars, faculty and trustees — and my full name announced as the signature. All the rest of us are to do the same."

"What is supposed to be the object?" inquired Abbie.

"That's exactly what bothered us, until Mr. Hammond announced the reason. He said it was to discover how many of us, after using our best writing skills, would write a letter that after two years we would be willing to acknowledge as ours."

Ester sat up with flushed cheeks. "That's a wonderful idea," she said, clapping her hands together happily. "I'm so glad you told me about it. Sadie, I'll write a letter for you to keep for that day. I'll write it tomorrow, and you are to keep it sealed until the evening of the day you graduate. Then when you have come up to your room and are alone, you are to read it. Will you promise, Sadie?"

Sadie laughed. "You're growing sentimental, Ester, as sure as the world. How can I make any such promise as that? I shall probably chatter to you like a magpie instead of reading anything."

She had ignored Ester's illness as much as she could and never permitted anyone to speak in her presence of their fears concerning the end result. Ester had stopped trying to convince her, so now she only smiled and repeated her request.

"Will you promise, Sadie?"

"Oh, yes, I'll promise to go to the mountains of the moon on foot and alone, across fields — anything to entertain you. I'll do anything to get you over this absurd habit of cuddling down among the pillows."

A few days later she received with apparent joy the letter which had been sealed and addressed to her and dropped it in her writing desk. Before she turned the key, a tear or two fell on the shining lid.

As the hot summer days waxed long and fierce, the invalid continued to droop, and the faces in the home grew sadder. From time to time those days of rallying still appeared, and Sadie confidently pronounced her to be improving rapidly. And so it came to pass that the words of a wonderful old poem proved to be a fitting description of the final communication, so sweet it was.

> They thought her dying when she slept,
> And sleeping when she died.

Into the brightness of the September days one intruded into the house with that strange, solemn stillness that comes only to those homes where death has left its seal. Long crepe bands floated from the doors. Those who had come to take their parting look at the white, tranquil face were gathering in the great parlors. "ESTER RIED, age 19," the coffin plate told them. Thus early the story of her life had been finished.

Ester had made only one arrangement for this last scene in her life's drama.

"I'm going to preach my own funeral service," she had said pleasantly to Abbie one day. "I want everyone to know what was the most important thing in life to me. And I want them to understand that when I came to the end of my life it remained the most important thing — for Christians, I mean. My sermon is to be preached for them. No, it isn't either; it applies to everyone. The last time I went to the city I found in a bookstore just the kind of message I want preached. I bought it. You'll find the package in my top bureau drawer, Abbie. I leave it to you to see that they are placed so that everyone who comes to look at me will be sure to see them."

So on this day amid the wilderness of flowers and vines and mosses that had taken possession of the rooms, beautifully illuminated texts hung in clusters on the walls and along the mantel. Among them were these verses, which spoke volumes to the mourners who gathered silently in the parlors:

And that knowing the time, that now it is

high time to awake out of sleep.

Whatsoever thy hand findeth to do, do it with thy might; for there is no work, nor device, nor knowledge, nor wisdom in the grave whither thou goest.

Awake thou that sleepest, and arise from the dead, and Christ shall give thee light.

The voice of the minister joined in with the thoughts of those who knew who had directed that the texts be displayed. "And I heard a voice from heaven saying unto me, Write, Blessed are the dead which die in the Lord from henceforth: Yea, saith the Spirit, that they may rest from their labors; and their works do follow them."

So Ester Ried, lying quietly in her coffin, was counted among that number who "being dead, yet speaketh."

CHAPTER XXVIII

AT LAST

he exciting celebration was over. Sadie Ried was no longer a school girl; she had graduated. A dress of the softest, purest white had been substituted for the blue silk, in which she had so long ago meant to appear. Its simple folds had swept the platform of Music Hall in as triumphant a way as she had ever intended for the other. More so, Sadie's wildest dreams had never made her valedictorian of her class, yet she certainly was.

In some ways it had been a joyous day. The letters that had been sealed for two years were opened and read by their respective holders. Laughing and blushing, the young ladies had discovered that many of the words they had carefully written only two years before were "ridiculously out of place" or "absurdly sentimental."

"Progress," said Mr. Hammond, turning for a moment to Sadie. He had watched with amusement the changing expression on her face, while she listened to the reading of her letter. "You didn't realize you had improved so much in two years, now, did you?"

"I didn't know I was ever such a simpleton!" she replied, at once provoked and amused.

Tonight Sadie was loitering in the parlors, in the halls and on the stairs, chatting aimlessly with anyone who would stop. It was growing late. Mrs. Ried and the children had gone to bed earlier. Dr. Van Anden hadn't yet returned from his evening round of calls. Everybody in and about the house was quiet, before Sadie, with slow, reluctant steps, finally climbed the stairs and sought her room.

Once there, she took her time in lighting the gas. The rays of the moon streamed into the room. She sat down in front of one of the low windows to enjoy it. But from there she could see the nearby cemetery and the gleaming marble slab on which was engraved the letters she knew so well: "Ester, daughter of Alfred and Laura Ried, died September 4, 18 — , age 19. Asleep in Jesus — Awake to everlasting life."

That reminded her, although she had no need to be reminded, of a letter with the seal unbroken, lying in her writing desk. She had promised to read that letter this evening — promised the one who wrote it for her and over whose grave the moonlight was now wrapping its silver robe.

Sadie recoiled from reading that letter. She could imagine its contents. She was still "halting between two opinions," "almost persuaded" — still on that often fatal "almost" side, instead of the "altogether." So she had lingered and frittered away the evening as best she could, rather than face that solemn letter.

Even when she turned bravely from the window

and lighted the gas and pulled down the shade, she waited to put everything in order on her writing table. She unlocked her writing desk and read over half a dozen old letters and bits of essays and scraps of poetry. Finally she reached down for that little white envelope with her name traced by the dear familiar hand that wrote her name no more. At last the seal was broken, and Sadie read:

My darling sister:

I am sitting today in our little room — yours and mine. I have been taking in the picture of it. Everything about it is dear to me, from our father's face smiling down on me from the wall, to the little red rocker in which he sat and wrote. I'm sitting in it now, and you will probably sit in it, when I have gone to him.

I want to speak to you about that time. When you read this, I shall have been gone a long, long time, and the bitterness of the parting will be past. You'll be able to read calmly what I'm writing. I'll tell you a little of the struggle.

For the first few moments after I knew I was going to die soon, my mind fairly reeled; it seemed to me that I could not. I had so much to live for; there was so much that I wanted to do. And most of all I wanted to see you a Christian. I wanted to live for that, to work for it, to undo if I could some of the evil that I knew my miserable life had brought to your heart.

Then suddenly the thought came to me that perhaps what my life could not

do, my coffin would — perhaps that was
to be God's way of calling you to Himself. Perhaps He meant to answer my
pleading in that way, to let my grave
speak for me, as my crooked, marred,
sinful living might never be able to do.
My darling, I was content then. It came to
me so suddenly that God meant to use
me thus. I love you so, and I long so to
see you come to Him that I am more than
willing to give up all that this life seemed
to have for me and go away, if by that
you would be called to Christ.

And, Sadie, dear, you will know before
you read this, how much I had to give
up. You will know very soon all that Dr.
Douglass and I looked forward to being
to each other, although it was just bud-
ding. But I give it up, give him up, more
than willingly — joyfully — glad that my
Father will accept the sacrifice and make
you His child.

Oh, my darling, what a life I have
lived before you! I don't wonder that,
looking at me, you have thought there is
nothing in religion. You have looked at
me, not at Jesus, and there has been no
reflection of His beauty in me. The result
is not unexpected.

Knowing this, I'm even more thankful
that God will forgive me and use me as a
means to bring you home at last. I'm
speaking confidently. I'm sure, you see,
that it will come about. The burden of
fear that I've carried about for so long
has disappeared. My Redeemer and

yours has taken it from me. I will see you in heaven. Father is there, and I am going, oh, so fast, and Mother will not be long behind. Alfred and Julia have started on the journey, and you will start. Oh, I know it — we shall all be there!

I told the Lord I was willing to do anything, anything, so that the awful mockery of a Christian life I wore for so long might not be the means of your eternal death. And He has heard my prayer. I don't know when it will be. Perhaps you will still be undecided when you sit in our room and read these words. Oh, I hope you won't waste two years more of your life. But if you do, if, as you read these my last lines, the question is unsettled, I charge you by the memory of your beloved sister not to wait another moment — not one. Oh, my darling, let me beg this at your hands. Take it as my dying petition, renewed after two years of waiting. Come to Jesus now.

With that question settled, then let me give you one word of warning. Do not live as I have done. My life has been a failure — five years of stupid sleep, while the enemy waked and worked. Oh, God, forgive me! Sadie, never let that be your record. Let me give you a motto: "Press toward the mark." The mark is high. Don't get distracted from it or forget it, as I did. Don't be content with simply sauntering along, looking toward it now and then. Consider the full meaning of that sentence, and live it: "Press toward the mark!"

And now good-bye. When you finish reading this letter, do this last thing for me: If you are already a Christian, get down on your knees and renew your covenant. Resolve again to live and work and suffer and die for Christ. If you are not a Christian — oh, I put my whole soul into this last request — I beg you to kneel and give yourself up to Jesus. My darling, good-bye until we meet in heaven.

Your loving sister,
Ester

The letter dropped from Sadie's weak fingers. She arose softly, turned down the gas and raised the shade. The moonlight still gleamed on the marble slab. In the shadows she could see a man walking with quick, firm steps up the street and was startled as she recognized Dr. Van Anden. Her thoughts went to that other lonely doctor, who was to have been her brother, and then returned to the letter and the words, "I give him up." She realized, as only those who know by experience can, what a giving up that would be. How much her sister longed for her soul. Then moved by a firm resolve, Sadie knelt in the solemn moonlight. The long, long struggle was ended. Father and sister were in heaven, but on earth tonight their prayers were being answered.

Blessed are the dead which die in the Lord from henceforth: Yea, saith the Spirit, that they may rest from their labors; and their works do follow them.

OTHER BOOKS BY
ISABELLA MACDONALD ALDEN
IN THE ALDEN COLLECTION

———

The King's Daughter
A New Graft on the Family Tree
As in a Mirror

Available from:

Creation House
190 North Westmonte Drive
Altamonte Springs, FL 32714
(407) 862-7565